I0676690

CHECK THE SPECIMEN

Antics in the outpatient lab

A novel by
Rebecca Osborn

This book is a work of fiction. Any similarities to real people or places is purely coincidental.

Copyright © Rebecca Osborn 2020. All rights reserved.

Printed in the United States of America.

Cover design: Susan Schreiner

ISBN 978-0-578-68373-7 (paperback)

CHAPTER

SOME PEOPLE ARE BLESSED with patience and that makes them well equipped to deal with medical patients. I am not one of those people. I have to keep all of my fingers and toes crossed all day long, hoping to get through the day without my manager calling me saying there was a problem. My name is Betty and I am the lead phlebotomist here at SuperLab. I work with two other phlebotomists, Liz and Dotty, and our job is to draw blood from patients for medical testing.

Phlebotomy is a field where we deal with people daily who are nervous, stressed and in a rush to get in and out of our lab as quickly as possible. To help us cope we try to do things to lighten things up where we can. If we can manage to make it fun the day goes by faster. Lately every day at SuperLab makes me feel like I am in the Twilight Zone.

It starts the second I unlock the front door for the first patient.

Our lab is located inside the Whitney Park Health Center

in Whitney Park, California. We have an Urgent Care unit at one end of the building and a Primary Care office at the other end. We are right in the middle of the hall, this makes for lots of patients and lots of problems.

"Good morning" I say as I unlock the door and hold it open for the first few patients. "Ma'am how long is this going to take?" says the first old lady. "I need to eat right away or I might drop dead right here on the floor." I ask everyone to please sign in and have a seat, and let them know that I will try and get them all in and out as quickly as possible. There are ten people in line. I hear a commotion. I see two old ladies using their walkers to try and jockey for the front of the line. Crap, the bigger one just knocked the smaller one down and she is bleeding profusely. Not a good way to start the day.

Meanwhile my coworker Liz just arrived. I ask her if she can tend to the mess in the waiting room. People are just stepping over the lady on the floor because they want to get to the front of the line.

I call the first patient. "Have you been in to SuperLab before?" "Yes, a couple of times." "Okay, may I see your insurance cards please?" As she is digging through her wallet I make a general announcement asking people to please have their insurance cards ready. I get her signed in and place her requisition form on the counter after making sure she has fasted, her lab tests require that she had no food since midnight.

In the meantime I am looking for our third phlebotomist who should be here already. "Where is Dotty?" I holler to Liz. I am reminded that she never arrives before nine fifteen a.m.

I see Mr. Brown is here for his Protime. Patients who are on blood thinners' require a Protime test be done regularly to make sure their blood is not too thin. "Good morning Mr.

Brown" I say as he struggles with his cane to get to the window. I notice he has just knocked over the display of cards at the window. "Okay, I have your billing information, you can go ahead and have a seat" I say. "Why the hell didn't you tell me that before I walked all the way up here?" he says. At this point things are moving along fairly well, it is nine sixteen a.m. and Dotty has just honored us with her presence.

Dotty heads straight to the back room and sets up the Scrabble board. One of the ways we get through the day here at SuperLab is to keep a Scrabble game going in the back room. Whenever we get a break we go to the back room to take our turn. Dotty walks out and says "when you get a chance can you *check the specimen?*" That is our code for *it is your turn.*

The phone rings and it is the nurse from the Urgent Care unit at the end of the hall. They need someone to come down and draw some blood, STAT, which means immediately. I send Dotty down the hall and I keep registering patients. Liz is drawing and processing the blood. It is very important that the blood be drawn and processed correctly. If there is a mistake the results could be inaccurate and it could effect the patients health.

After the blood is drawn the tubes have to sit for fifteen to twenty minutes, then we have to place the tube in a centrifuge and spin it for another fifteen minutes. There is a piece of wax-like stuff in the tube and when it is spun it separates the serum from the rest of blood. The serum portion of the blood is what the test is generally done on. The tubes are then sent to our main lab via courier where the final testing is completed.

The phone is ringing again and this time it is Joan at the Primary Care office at the other end of the hall saying "Doctor

Sweeney is looking for results on several patients." I tell her one of us will be down shortly. Meanwhile I call the main lab to tell them to send a courier to pick up the STAT.

I hear Liz holler "Cedrick is here." "Okay" I say. She can see him through the window. He always stops to pee on the front of the building. His wife Mary stands patiently waiting for him to finish. "Good morning Cedrick" I say as he waddles in the front door. His wife grabs a magazine and looks happy to just have a break. I am grabbing the lab results off the printer to take down the hall to Doctor Sweeney. All of a sudden the printer starts going nuts and is reprinting everything again and then again. I am looking around for cameras thinking surely this must be a joke. I stumble down the hall with the results. As I approach the window Joan says "whew just in time." Doctor Sweeney says he wants those results here before nine a.m. no exceptions. I make a mental note to keep playing the Lottery. I smile and say "have a nice day."

I tell Liz to please *check on the specimen.* Her turn in our ongoing Scrabble game in the back room. "SuperLab" I say as I grab the phone. "Hi this is Jackie in Urgent Care. Any idea how long before we get the results on that STAT?" "Well Dotty just now has it spinning and we are waiting for the courier to pick it up and take it to the main lab. I am guessing a few hours." "What? That is unacceptable."

I say "can you hold please?" I yell "Liz it's for you!" I hear her pick up the extension and I giggle to myself. The least she can do is take this call since I now have to draw Cedrick's blood. "Good morning Mr. Murphy. How are you today?" "Well not too bad but I am never going back to that doctor." I know I really shouldn't ask but I say "oh really, why is that?" Well he made me wait forever and then he stuck his finger up my butt." "Oh my" I said. "Well I am sure he had a good reason right?" "I don't think so. I am perfectly fine except I can't pee." I finish up and tape his arm and tell him to have a nice day.

I take Mr. Murphy's blood to the back only to discover Liz holding our tube of blood that is a STAT from Urgent Care. Liz says "this blood is hemolyzed." This can happen for various reasons and has to do with how the blood was collected. If the red blood cells have been broken the serum portion of the blood is red instead of looking like apple juice. This can make certain tests results inaccurate.

The serum portion of the blood from most people looks like apple juice. Some people have too much fat in their blood, causing the serum to look like milk. Usually that means their triglycerides are very high.

We cannot send this to the main lab for processing. Someone has to go redraw the patient. We agree that it has to be one of us, not Dotty. I call Urgent Care. "Hi Bill this is Betty down in the lab. We need to redraw Mr. Jones because his blood sample is hemolyzed." Bill tells me to hold on for a minute while he checks with the doctor. "Hi Betty, listen, the doctor just sent Mr. Jones to the hospital by ambulance, so just forget the whole thing. They will draw his blood there." I say "okay fine." Great, just wasted twenty minutes I say to myself.

I walk to the front desk as the courier walks in the door. "Hi Tim, how is it going?" "I am super tired." "Oh really how come?" "I was up late texting with my new girlfriend." "Okay hang on and I will get you all the specimens that I have so you did not waste a trip. That STAT was canceled." I go to the back to get the specimens to give him.

I head up to the front with the samples. "Liz have you seen our courier? He was just here." I start looking around from room to room. Nothing. I knock on bathroom door. Tim are you in there? Nothing. The door is locked.

I keep knocking but get no answer. I honestly am starting to regret coming into work today. I call Urgent Care asking if anybody down there has a spare key to our bathroom door. I am put on hold. Meanwhile two other calls come in and I place them on hold. Bill from Urgent Care comes back on the phone and says he has a key and will be right down. I go up to the front counter and Liz says "that was Sheryl that you put on hold, and she is really pissed off and wants you to call her back." Oh lovely, this is not going to end well. Sheryl is our supervisor at the main lab. Sheryl is clueless as to how over-worked we are down here.

Bill walks in with the key and heads for the bathroom. Dotty is busy with a difficult draw and apparently Liz just scooted into the back room to *check the specimen*, her turn in our ongoing Scrabble game. So it looks like I am it. I get to assist Bill.

I can hear someone at the front counter ringing the bell repeatedly.

Bill opens the bathroom door and there is Tim on the floor with his pants around his ankles sound asleep. I offer Bill five bucks to take care of this problem.

Okay, I head up to the front office to see who is ringing the bell incessantly? There stands Cedrick with blood running all over his arm and dripping down his elbow onto the carpet. The good news is this blood sort of blends in with the blood from the lady who fell earlier. "Hello Mr. Murphy come on back here and lets get you cleaned up."

Patients who come in for a Protime are usually on a blood thinner drug called Coumadin. The lab has to check the level of the medication in the patients blood so their blood does not get too thin. We repeat the same words to each patient. "Leave the bandage on and do not lift anything for a few minutes." Mr. Murphy has trouble following directions. He is several cans short of a six pack.

I hold some pressure on his arm for several minutes as I ask him what happened? "Well, I was walking out to the car and stopped at the drinking fountain. I pushed the button on the fountain and the water starting flowing up towards the ceiling. Luckily I am very smart. I took off my bandage and shoved the cotton into the hole in the water fountain to slow down the flow and now it works just fine."

I can not believe he stuck his bloody cotton bandage in the drinking fountain and people are drinking out of that fountain! Well I am not being paid to fix that problem. I think I shall keep this one to myself and carry on. I cannot believe it is not quite lunch time yet. I need to ask for a raise.

CHAPTER

I DECIDE TO REFILL MY WATER BOTTLE before calling our supervisor Sheryl back. I head down to Urgent Care, the only place in the building to get filtered water right now. As I return to the office and head to my desk to call Sheryl Liz says "thyroid baby is here," which alerts me not to take any other patients.

This little one is an infant that was born with a thyroid condition that requires her to come into the lab once a week for blood work. When she arrives the mother is already upset and crying and we try to take care of her as soon as possible.

It takes two of us to draw an infant, one to hold the baby and one to draw the blood. Liz says "I have a major sinus headache, I can hold, if you draw the baby." "Sure no problem."

Again I am thinking I need a huge raise in pay and make a mental note to ask Sheryl about this when I call her back.

Okay we get the baby done and I take the blood to the back and Liz is bandaging the baby and trying to soothe the mother.

I hear a few words of the conversation and decide not to go back into the room. Apparently the baby's mother was sobbing and saying it hurts her feelings when we refer to her baby as the *thyroid baby*. We agree to be careful not to use that phrase in front of the mother in the future.

Liz comes out to get more aspirin out of her purse and says "you owe me." I laugh and tell her it is her turn to *check the specimen*.

I sit down and call Sheryl for another ass chewing.

"Hi Sheryl this is Betty in Whitney Park returning your call." "Listen" she says "I called over an hour ago, what the hell is going on down there? I just received a call from a patient saying there was a man on the floor of the bathroom with no pants on." Oh crap I say to myself this is not good. "Just a minor incident but it is all taken care of now" I assure her. I have started referring to all of our disasters as incidents.

"So Betty how are things going down there?" "Not too bad" I say as I think to myself there must be something in the drinking water in Whitney Park. Usually things are worse when there is a full moon, but every day feels like it is a full moon here inside SuperLab. Betty, do you think you could send Dotty down here for the afternoon? I am thinking, she is always late, rarely gets the patients blood on the first stick, and moves like a turtle so why the hell not. "Sure, no problem" I say.

I did not remind her that Liz leaves at two p.m. and I would be alone the last three hours. She should know this as it has been the norm now for three years.

"I am going to lunch" I say to Liz. I change clothes and get ready to go hit some tennis balls across the street at the park. I hear it is supposed to be a great stress reliever. After tennis I make a quick stop at the store for something I will be able to eat at my desk in the afternoon. The plan is to head down to Urgent Care where I can shower and get my scrubs back on, making me only about fifteen minutes over my allotted one hour lunch break. Since I rarely get to take any other breaks during the day I feel this is fair.

I head for the back door to Urgent Care and slip into the on call room to the shower. I strip and head for the shower. Well imagine my surprise when I open the door to find Jackie and Bill already in the shower, together. So there I stand, naked and sweaty. Luckily Bill had his back to me and Jackie seems happily preoccupied.

I quietly close the door and use the sink for a little sponge bath. I hurry and dry off, jump into my scrubs and beat it out of there as quickly as possible. I smile at the nurse as I walk down the hall like it was just another day. Geeze Louise this place gets crazier each year.

Okay, I am back at SuperLab and it's time to eat my lunch at the desk while I work. Liz walks out and says when you get a chance you may want to *check that specimen*.

I ask if the courier has been here yet? "Just left" Liz says. Great now all I have to do is stay caught up. Apparently Liz is headed to go get the mail. I slip into the back room to *check the specimen*. I can see Liz is kicking my ass at our ongoing Scrabble game so I make a few changes. I turned a couple of my letters over to be blanks which I can use for anything. I am thinking this should help me pull ahead.

I finish with my turn and head up front to take my spot

at the window. Liz walks in with an armful of mail including *stool cards* that have been completed. We routinely give patients these occult blood cards when we draw their blood. The occult blood cards are to check for blood in the patients stools. We give the patients very specific instructions on how to best complete the cards. Probably three out of one hundred patients actually listen and understand what to do. They are then supposed to mail them back in.

Okay, so now Liz is on her way out the door since her day is over at two p.m. Of course she has to do her usual routine. She pokes her head in the door as she walks out and says "see ya wouldn't want to be ya."

I usually laugh but today I just ignore her. Oh joy, I get to open the mail. Since this is not my first rodeo I have learned to wear gloves when opening the stool cards. First I open the regular mail, then the stool cards. As usual several of our elderly patients have placed the smear of stool on the outside of the cards instead of on the inside. The instructions are really very easy, all the patients have to do is just turn the toilet paper upside down and put a little smear in each window on the inside of the opened card. Close the card, then put your name and date of birth on the outside and send it back in the mail. Very simple. Well, now I can see Mrs. Brown only put her name on the outside of the envelope not on the card, and smeared the stool on the outside of the cards. What a lovely project to do right after your last bite of lunch.

I see four more cards with the same problem. I just bag them up to go with the courier to the main lab.

I see three patients coming inside to have their blood drawn. The fun is beginning. Sometimes Liz calls to see how busy it is, just to rub it in that she is home watching TV.

I get busy and get these patients done. I start processing the blood and getting it ready for the courier. Some of the blood gets spun down in the centrifuge and the serum needs to be poured off into a plastic tube and frozen, this all depends on which test is ordered. The serum is on top in the SST tube. As the blood spins in the centrifuge the blood separates in the tube.

My job is to have everything ready for the courier at four fifty five p.m. Right now I am feeling pretty good about being almost caught up.

The phone rings and it is Urgent Care. They need a draw done STAT. Right now. Before I head down with my tray to do the draw I take the phone and put both lines on hold and put the phone in the drawer. Then I hide my purse. Okay, down the hall to Urgent Care I go. If patients come in while I am gone they will be waiting awhile.

As I arrive at Urgent Care Mary is sitting at the desk and says the draw is in room two. I see Jackie is in the room with the patient. I try and act normal and not think of me seeing her in the shower with Bill. Well the patient is a two-year-old with a fever and sore throat. I ask Jackie if she can hold? She says okay. Mom is crying and Dad is pacing the floor. My favorite type of draw!

Twenty minutes later I am headed back to the lab with the blood. As I walk in the front door six patients are looking mighty unhappy. I ask if they can please sign in and I will be right with them. "We signed in twenty minutes ago" one of them yells. I get the blood going in the centrifuge, dig the phone out of the drawer and call the main lab asking them to send the courier to pick up the STAT draw.

One of these patients is a drug screen which is complicated. I do the paperwork on the first patient and call her back to sit in the draw chair. Meanwhile, the guy with the drug screen says he has to go now.

I quickly do the paperwork and give him instructions. While he is in the bathroom I draw the other woman real quick. This keeps people in the waiting room feeling like the line is moving and they will eventually be called.

I hear a commotion and as I peek around the corner I see a second young man slip out of the bathroom into the waiting room.

I tape the patient's arm and send her on her way. I make sure labels are on the tubes then rush to the bathroom as the young man walks out with his specimen. He is holding his specimen. I check the cup and it is barely warm and not registering on the temperature gauge on the cup. This is a problem. This means his buddy brought in urine from the outside for him to use.

I say "wait a minute I just saw somebody else come out of the bathroom. Where did he go?" I quickly open door to the lobby to check. Nobody in the lobby, but I see the guy out in the hall through the glass window. I ask to see the patient's ID again. I verify the picture then I ask him to have a seat in the waiting room for a moment. I go to the back room while holding on to his ID. I call the main lab and ask Sheryl for instructions on how to handle this situation. She instructs me to send him up to the main lab with his paperwork.

This happens when somebody has to have a drug screen done and they know it will come back showing they are still using. They sometimes try and sneak someone else in with a clean urine. So I send him off to the main lab. He was still denying sneaking his friend into the bathroom when he left.

I head back to front desk to call the next patient. I look at the clock. Four p.m. Only one more hour until this day finally ends. The courier walks in as I am calling the next patient up to the window. I excuse myself and go get the STAT for Brandon, the courier. I give him everything that I have processed. Brandon says another courier will be back at five p.m. Very good.

I head back to the window to my next patient who by now is quite irritated. "Are you always alone?"

I say yes, from two to five p.m. I am alone. I have been waiting thirty minutes here and I have things to do. I say "I understand." "Well I want to talk to your supervisor." "Okay, no problem" I say as I hand her the name and number. I say "have a nice day" as she waddles out.

Great, now I will be hearing from Sheryl sometime in the next two days. I draw five more patients and keep the processing going. You have to keep up with it if you want any hope of getting out of this place on time.

I keep my fingers crossed that nobody walks in at four fiftyfive p.m. Seriously, what are people thinking walking into the lab five minutes before it closes? I turn the lights off in the waiting room at four fifty p.m. hoping nobody will come in. It appears my luck is holding. The courier arrives and I give her all the specimens and thankfully this day is finally over.

I head for my car hoping it starts, God forbid I get stuck here. Just thinking about tomorrow reminds me to stop and buy a lottery ticket on the way home.

CHAPTER

WELL HERE I GO AGAIN, another day starting. I have a forty minute drive to the lab. I have everything in my purse and car to survive for awhile.

I get to the first stoplight and look in the mirror. Huge mistake. My hair doesn't look right. Oh no, this morning I was in such a hurry to get ready, get my scrubs on and head to the lab that I forgot to rinse the cream rinse out of my hair. I am fishing around with one hand while I drive, looking for the roll of paper towels. I feel lucky they are still here. I am now driving with one hand and using my other hand to sop up all the cream rinse out of my hair.

I am afraid I will use most of the roll of towels. Luckily this traffic light is long enough to plant a garden. I am using both hands now, desperate to get the cream rinse out of my hair. I look up and realize the light is green. Apparently the man next to me at the light has thoroughly enjoyed watching me.

I arrive and am now trying to comb and brush my hair so it is somehow acceptable. I get the door to SuperLab open and the lights turned on. There are five people waiting. I say "good morning everyone." I grab my lab coat and put my things away and get the machines turned on. I was the last person to *check the specimen* yesterday, so now it is Dotty's turn.

I call the first patient up to the window and get her registered. I register three more patients before I start drawing the blood. I see Fred and Martha Owens are here. I say "hello" and let them know I will be with them as soon as I can. Okay Liz has just arrived. Things will pick up now. I see Liz is drawing blood now too. I decide to go process the blood in the back.

I say "hi" to Liz. She does not seem to be her usually cheerful self. Liz says "what happened to your hair?"

"I had a little incident, you will not believe it" I say as I head to the back. "I woke up irritated this morning. It made me feel rushed and I forgot to rinse the cream rinse out of my hair. Last night on my way home I decided to stop and rent a movie. Well, I was told that my renting privilege had been revoked. I was shocked and embarrassed. So I found out that my eighteen year old son Jared and his girlfriend Brianna rented some movies on my account and never returned them. Liz gives me a look like "oh yes, I believe it."

I start the centrifuge and I hear Liz on the phone with somebody and she sounds annoyed. Liz yells "Betty it's for you." I pick the phone up saying "this is Betty may I help you?" A mans' voice says "like I said, I am at the traffic light where are you?" I stick my head around the corner and look at Liz who is laughing and looking quite pleased as she says "gotcha."

"Sir," I say in my nicest voice, "there are approximately one hundred traffic lights in Whitney Park, which one are you at?" "Oh," silence. "I can't see the sign can you hang on while I move up a little?" Seriously? I say to myself. "Sure I can wait." Well twenty minutes later we figure out where he is and I can finally hang up. I say "we will see you shortly."

It looks like we are fairly caught up. As I walk out front here comes Steffy. She is a phlebotomist who travels around to various outpatient offices filling in wherever needed. She looks like a poorly made up beauty contestant. She has bright red hair this week and long bright red fingernails to match. I say hello and ask who sent her? Apparently Sheryl sent her to fill in for Dotty. Great, now Liz and I will not be able to relax and talk in between patients. Liz is drawing someone in another room as I sit down at the front desk and call the next patient to the window. He hobbles up to the window.

I can hear Steffy on her phone in another room talking loudly. Apparently she is having a disagreement with her boyfriend. This relationship has been going on since I met her two years ago.

I go back to my new patient Larry Johnson. I ask for his insurance information and his date of birth. When I ask for his date of birth he says "no thank you." I said "this question is not optional." He asks "why do you need to know that?" I explain that we need it to look him up in our system. He says oh "so I cannot get my blood drawn if I do not tell you my date of birth?" I just shake my head for yes. At this point I am afraid to speak because something nasty may pop out of my mouth.

He reluctantly gives me the information and says "I called on the phone, I had trouble finding this place." Next I ask him if he is fasting? "Pretty much" he says. I ask "is that a yes or no?" I can tell by looking at the tests on his lab slip that he needs to be fasting. As he starts to turn around and have a seat he says "have you ever had those new sausage McGriddles? I just had three of them." Now I am getting irritated. I said "oh so this is a pseudo fast?" I get no reply. I just smile and say "okay, have a seat and someone will call you back soon."

I grab a sticky pad off the stack and place Liz's name on it and put his requisition in the pile. This makes it look like he knew her and requested her. Now I am quite tickled with myself. Gotcha back! If the patient is difficult over the phone and at the window there is a very good chance that it will be worse when you get them in the back to draw their blood.

I stand up and tell Steffy I am taking results down the hall and will be right back. I asked her if she can keep the processing going while I am gone. As Steffy heads for my chair I am watching her thinking holy cow, she is not wearing anything under her lab coat. Well this is a new low even for her. Wait til I tell Liz. Nobody was at the desk at the Primary Care office so I leave the results on the desk.

As I walk back into our office and head through the lobby into the back I hear Liz having an interesting conversation with a man in her draw chair.

As I get closer I can hear her trying to explain how to collect Ova and Parasite stool collections in the bottles to our new patient Larry Johnson. This test requires the patient put a certain amount of stool into two different bottles, then put their name and date of birth on the bottles and return them to the lab for processing. I saw her stick her head around the corner and mouth a not so nice comment to me. I laughed all the way to the Scrabble game in back.

As Liz comes out of her draw room I say "when you get a chance can you *check that specimen?*" She will be most unhappy as I just used the Z on a triple letter spot for two words in our ongoing Scrabble game.

As Liz was headed for the processing room she motioned for me to follow her.

She says "do you have any idea what Steffy is wearing under her lab coat?" I said "no, but to me it looked like not much of anything." We decide Liz will take a break and I will see if I can find out.

As I walk out I observe Steffy trying to tie a tourniquet onto some poor man's arm and it appears that one of her big long nails has gotten stuck in with the tourniquet and has come off her finger. The tourniquet is like a flat wide rubber band that we tie around the patient's arm, it makes it easier to find a vein. I had to turn away so I would not laugh.

I hear her call for help. With Liz not here I pretty much have to go help. As I walk in the door I see a long red nail hanging from the tourniquet. She says "I am having difficulty here can you hand me the tubes?"

The poor male patient has a please help me look on his face. Okay, so we get through the mess and send the patient on his way. I bet he calls Sheryl at the main lab with a complaint.

I am thinking it is almost time for lunch. Liz and I both are fairly quick at drawing the blood but it takes Steffy twenty minutes to draw one patient. I think those fake red nails are going to be a problem.

I decide that I would run to the grocery store for a few things and bag them up tight and stick them in the refrigerator so I don't have to stop after work. Then I will stop at the cheap Chinese place over in a strip mall and get us each a two item plate. So we have Steffy working on drawing a few patients while Liz and I get the lunch order done and the money collected.

As I am heading out the door for lunch I hear Steffy asking Liz if she can leave when Betty gets back because it is too hard to draw blood with one nail missing. I gave her a you have got to be kidding look and Liz did pretty much the same thing.

As the door closes I hear Steffy telling Liz the whole sordid story of how her nail came off. I think I will drag my feet a bit while running my errands.

At the store I grab a cart and get a few things. I only have two more things to get in the produce section. I look up as I hear a woman's voice saying "hi do you remember me?" I am thinking hell no. She says "I have to confess I was thinking of my anniversary coming up when you were explaining to me how to collect stool samples for those cards. Can you remind me again?" I could not think of a way out of this one. So people are looking at us standing next to the oranges talking about stool card collection. This is ridiculous!

I arrived at the cheap Chinese restaurant and discovered eight people in front of me. Wonderful! Of course I am thinking standing in line here beats being in the office.

As I return to the office, where we are ready to start gorging ourselves on Chinese food, I hear Steffy telling Liz the whole story of why she had to wear only skimpy underwear under her lab coat. I listen from the break room while I unpack our Chinese food. Liz was looking bored to tears.

Apparently Steffy had gone straight to her boyfriend's after work where they had a major fight. She said he was throwing her out and all she could grab was her lab coat and underwear. He had her keys so she had to dig through her purse for an extra car key, unfortunately he still has her apartment key. Liz looked relieved when I yelled lunch.

Steffy offers to watch the front window while we go in the back to play Scrabble and eat. I can hear Steffy on the phone with the girl who did her nails. Steffy likes her nails and hair to match. She was trying to explain how her nail came off and the young girl at the salon had no idea what a tourniquet was. Steffy will have to pay for it to be fixed. Liz will be leaving at two p.m., so it will be a very long three hours working with Steffy.

Steffy sticks her head in the door of the break room saying she was getting backed up and could use some help. Liz asks if I have any idea who hired her? I said I didn't.

It is time for Liz to leave for the day and as she is heading through the lobby to the door she comments loudly that we are down to one magazine again in the lobby. Seriously? I just brought in a stack of magazines a few days ago.

Liz says her usual "see ya wouldn't want to be ya" as she heads out the door. I give her a despondent look and mumble to myself "just shoot me now."

I register a patient who is in her motorized scooter. Steffy asks if I can draw her blood. I agree to do it. This lady does not look like she would be up to an adventure with Steffy.

I ask the lady if she can walk in to the draw chair? She says "yes, if someone can hold onto me." Okay I go to the door going into the lobby and help her back. I ask her if she thinks she can collect a urine sample for me after I draw her blood? She doesn't know. I go and get her a glass of water to sip. She looks a bit dehydrated. This is very common.

I am now checking each arm looking for the best vein when I hear what sounds like a bus load of people out in the lobby. I know Steffy is at the desk so I continue on.

After drawing the elderly woman's blood I have her hold pressure on the bandage for a few minutes while I finish labeling the tubes. I ask her to finish her water so she can get me a urine specimen. Suddenly I hear a loud crash. I stick my head out to see what was going on. A woman, with three young kids, has come in for lab work. Steffy was getting ready to draw the mother's blood.

We have one draw chair up in the front and then two other rooms each containing draw chairs. The mother was screaming at the children to settle down while she was seated in the front draw chair. I went to the waiting room to investigate. I cannot believe this is happening.

The sweet little old lady left her scooter in the lobby and two of the kids are on the scooter with the bigger one driving it around the lobby. Now they have crashed into our new water cooler and the jug of water has fallen off. There is water is everywhere.

This water cooler is a brand new addition to our office, Sheryl's idea. I yell for the kids to get off the scooter right now. I check to see how much longer the mother will be tied up? She is almost done. I manage to get the mostly empty water bottle back onto the cooler. I tell the kids to sit down and be quiet. The carpet is soaked.

I check on my patient to see if she is finished drinking her water and if she thinks she can get me a urine specimen. She says "pretty soon." "Okay" I tell her and let her know that I will be right back.

As I walk out, the mother is once again yelling at the kids.

Apparently she had three kids when she came in and now one is missing. I start checking rooms. Finally I try the bathroom door, it is locked and I hear water running. This is not good. There is a two year old playing in the bathroom with the door locked and the water running. At this point I am ready to wheel and deal if this woman promises never to return to our lab with these kids.

I call Urgent Care asking if Bill can bring the key to unlock the bathroom one more time. Now I am seeing water coming from under the door. Steffy tries to find towels to mop up the water. I go back into the blood draw room to explain to my patient it would just be a few minutes until the bathroom would be empty.

Here comes Bill with the key. As he opens the door we see a little boy sitting on the floor and he has emptied the soap dispenser onto the floor underneath the overflowing sink. I am in shock. It looks like a broken pipe has exploded in there. The mother comes running in and scoops the little boy up and gets him out of the bathroom. She says "I guess we better go now." "Do ya think?" I reply. Bill says he will be right back with a mop and towels.

I go back into the draw room and my patient says she is ready to give a urine sample now. I escort her to the bathroom and briefly give her a lame excuse as to why the floor is a mess and to please hold onto the bars and be careful. I wait for the lady to finish and get her back to her scooter and help her out the door. She does not appear to notice the water everywhere.

I go back to the front desk to sit down and relax before any more patients come in. Bill says he thinks he can get the mess cleaned up in the bathroom. I am so exhausted I just sit there staring at the wall. The good news is there is only one more hour until this day ends. Luckily it has been fifteen minutes with no patients coming in the door.

I asked Steffy to watch the front while I go down the hall to borrow some magazines to put in the waiting room. Actually I should not say borrow since they are not getting them back. We will be lucky if they last three days. These are not the best magazines by any stretch of the imagination but the patients' steal them just the same. The thought crosses my mind about bringing in horrible magazines that no patient would want to steal, however I am trying to avoid more calls from my supervisor Sheryl.

If she receives too many calls from patients complaining she makes me go over to the main lab or another office and work for awhile. Initially I hated working at the other labs, but I have gotten to know some of the other phlebotomists who are real characters, so it is not as bad as it used to be.

Most of the time our supervisor Sheryl is not there. She usually strolls in around one p.m. with her lunch from taco bell and goes into her office to answer phones.

When I work at the main lab it is quite interesting. There are a lot more patients, each with a different story. There is very little space so there are two draw stations in the hall-way. In the first draw room there are two chairs side by side with a partition in between. This gives the patient the illusion that there is some privacy. The person who is sitting in the first chair is literally up against the wall of the bathroom. This makes for all kinds of uncomfortable incidents.

Primary Care is running low on magazines so I head to Urgent Care to take a few of theirs.

As I return to our office I hear Steffy saying a quick good-bye to someone on the phone. "How did it go while I was gone?" I ask. "Pretty good, Joan from Primary Care came down looking for results on three patients." And you are telling me this because... I wonder. Steffy continues "I do not know how to look them up and print them out." I tell her to pull up a chair and we go through how to do this yet one more time.

We finish up and get the results printed out and I ask Steffy to please run them down to Joan at Primary Care. I am pretty sure I delivered those results to her earlier today. Sometimes they misplace them and then call to complain that they never received them. I think about making them sign for them but that would initiate a phone call complaining to Sheryl.

Here comes a patient through the door. I greet her with a friendly hello and a smile. She gives me her requisition. I ask for her insurance cards and her date of birth. She gave me a nasty look saying "young lady, don't you know it is not polite to ask an older lady her date of birth?"

Seriously? Why can't I just get a normal sweet lady? I try to be polite saying "ma'am I need this information to look you up in our system. I don't want to confuse you with someone else?" Suddenly she gets a panic look on her face. "What do you mean? You better not confuse me with anyone else. Are you new? How long have you been doing this?" She is starting to sweat. I think to myself how much fun it would be to pretend I was brand new and she was my first patient.

That is a really fun game we sometimes play with just the right type of patient. I could tell she would be absolutely the wrong patient for that game. "I have been doing this for twenty years" I say to her. "Well I hope you are good. My veins roll away and you are only getting one chance to get my blood." I love these types of patients at the end of my day. "Okay" I say, but I am thinking cool, one stick and I am done either way.

Steffy comes in and assesses the situation and goes to the back. I ask her if she can please work on the processing, as the courier will be here in thirty minutes.

I finish the paperwork and call this lovely patient back. Mrs. Nelson can you come on back now? I point to the draw chair where I want her to sit as she waddles in.

I typically put the tourniquet on both arms checking for the best vein for me to draw from. "Ouch, that tourniquet is so damn tight, do you need it that tight? I am afraid my arm will turn blue and fall off." No, I just put it extra tight because you were such a pain at the window I think to myself. "Sorry ma'am let me put it over your shirt so it will not hurt." I retie the tourniquet. I find the vein I will use and clean the spot with alcohol.

As I am uncapping the needle she says "why are you going there, they usually use that vein?" as she points to a different vein. "That vein does not feel as good to me" I say. "Well I want you to use this one" as she points to the vein I did not want to use. "Okay, if that is what you want me to do, but I do not feel a good vein there" I say. "Yes" she insists. Okay will do. So I clean her arm and stick the needle in and nothing. "Did you get it? Did you get it?" she says. I withdraw the needle and ask her to please hold pressure on the gauze, while I get the tape to tape her arm. "Okay" I say, "I was not able to get it from that vein, so here you go" I say as I hand her back her requisition with her tests listed on it.

"What's going on?" she says. "Here is the address of our main lab where you may go to have your blood drawn. They are open til six p.m. We are closing now." "Why are you stopping?" she says. "I used my one turn up and I used the vein you said but was unsuccessful" I say. "Ask for Bill over there he is pretty good and has lots of experience."

Just the thought of her asking for Bill makes me laugh out loud. This is another fun game we love to play. We send difficult patients to other offices, giving them the name of a phlebotomist that works there, who has lots of experience, but usually the phlebotomists that have a lot of experience have very little patience left. "Well you are being very rude" she says. "Okay, I must go prepare the specimens for transport with the courier" I say as I am exiting the draw room.

She glares at me as she walks out. I make a note on a sticky pad to put Mrs. Nelson on the list I have of patients who are difficult to deal with. I usually put Liz's name on their requisitions as if they had requested her. She does the same thing to me on a regular basis.

So here is Michelle, one of our couriers, my day is finally over. I think there is definitely something in the drinking water here in Whitney Park for sure. I am getting too many really strange people. The phone rings and I look at my watch. Five p.m. I let it go to the machine as I walk out the door.

CHAPTER

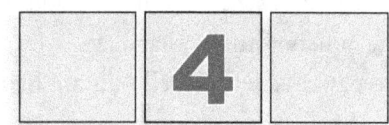

WELL THERE'S GOOD NEWS AND BAD NEWS. The good news is I woke up. The bad news is I did not win the lottery, so I must get showered and head to the lab to work. I wonder what kind of fun we will have in there today?

Maybe Liz will be in a good mood and we can play pranks on each other. The things we do to get through our work day! Well I think I need to start my day with some chocolate. I stop at the donut shop and get two chocolate donuts and a cup of coffee. Damn, I should do this every day, except then I would not be able to fit into my scrubs. I guess I could pull a Steffy and just wear my lab coat should my scrubs not fit anymore. I am really good at coming up with bad ideas.

As I arrive at the lab I see quite a few cars in the parking lot. I hope they are not all waiting at the door for the lab. The patients who need to fast usually show up right at eight a.m. and insist they are going to die if they don't eat right away.

Well there are only eight people waiting, not too bad. Every so often we get a smart patient who realizes they will not die if they fast and wait until nine a.m. after the initial line has gotten shorter.

As I approach the front door to unlock it there are two women having a conversation about whether or not it really matters whether or not you fast. Neither one is really sure what their tests are for. "Good morning ladies" I say as I unlock the door. Come on in, please sign in, have a seat and I will be right with you.

One lady drops her requisition on the floor and when she picks it up it is damp. She immediately says loudly "why is the carpet soaked in here?" I tell her there was an incident yesterday with the water cooler being knocked over. "It smells strange in here" she says. I make a mental note to call down the hall and see if they have one of those machines to vacuum up water. I check the answer machine while the last few patients sign in. There is a message from a patient Susan Jones complaining about the bruise on her arm. I make a note to call her back.

There is another message from Sheryl saying she needs to talk with me. I immediately wish I had called in sick. I write another note to call Sheryl. Last message is from Steffy saying she is supposed to be in at nine a.m. to fill in for Dotty but she has to get her nail fixed and will be late. Lovely. Time to call my first patient.

"Good morning Mr. Marshall" I say as he hobbles up to the window. I ask for his insurance card and ask if he is fasting? "Yes" he says. I have not even had a sip of water in over eight hours. I didn't even brush my teeth." I am thinking no kidding. His breath is about to knock me over. I see that he has a urinalysis marked, so I ask him if he would like to have a cup of water while he waits? I explain that is okay to have water while fasting.

I give Mr. Marshall a stack of cups to set on top of the water cooler. I tell him I will be with him shortly. I need to get the rest of the patients registered so when Liz gets here we can both be drawing blood.

I hear a lady who was at the end of the line yell "how come the line hasn't moved since I got here? I am starving and starting to feel weak." I assure her she will be fine and we will get to her as quickly as possible. I think I will ask Sheryl about maybe getting a Valium salt lick for the waiting room. I continue to register patients.

I take a sticky pad and put Liz's name on it and put it on top of the requisition for the darling little old lady who is complaining of being weak. This is my gift to Liz. Perfect way to start her day.

Okay Liz has just arrived. I call Mr. Marshall back. He immediately says he needs to lie down, because he tends to faint. I help him to the table to lie down. Phlebotomists would prefer that the patient tell us right up front if they need to lie down, rather than trying to scoop them off the floor later. He is fairly pleasant and I get his blood drawn quickly. I have him sit up slowly.

I ask him if he can get me a urine specimen? He says he needs to wait a few minutes. So I hand him a cup with his name on it, and explain where to set it when he is done. He returns to the waiting room.

The phone rings and it is Joan in Primary Care looking for results. I tell her I will be down shortly. So I draw a couple more patients, then I see Liz calling that darling woman in. I think this would be a good time to take results down the hall.

When I get back to the lab it looks fairly calm. Liz is still in her draw room with her special patient. I decide to go to the back room and *check the specimen*, take my turn in our ongoing Scrabble game. I decide to stick my head in the door to Liz's draw room and smile. She gives me a just you wait look. I laugh as I walk into our back room to take my turn. Okay all done with my turn. "Woo hoo" I just got over fifty points in one turn. Feeling pretty good I tell Liz I have to call Sheryl back and I need her to hold down the fort.

I call and get Sheryl on the phone. Betty, how are things down in Whitney Park? Well Sheryl, I am convinced there is something in the drinking water down here in Whitney Park. Sheryl laughs and says you may be right. "Betty, what was the story with Mrs. Nelson yesterday? She said you were rude and had no idea how to draw blood." I relayed all the sordid details to Sheryl about how difficult she was, and would only give me one chance to get her blood, and was telling me which vein to use. "Okay Betty, just try and be more patient in the future alright?" I assured her I would try.

"Oh Betty, one more thing. I just had a strange call from a patient saying the waiting room was wet and smells bad? What the hell was that all about?" "Well Sheryl, we had a minor incident down here yesterday." I relayed the details about the water cooler getting knocked over. Sheryl was laughing so hard I think she must have wet her pants. Seriously. "Let me send someone down to get the water vacuumed up" she offers. "Sheryl, I want to talk with you about getting a raise in pay." After the laughing stopped Sheryl said for me to stop by after work and talk to her about it. I said okay and we hang up. I settle in at the front desk and look up as Steffy comes flying in the door.

"I know I am late, but I couldn't help it" she says. "It is eleven fifteen a.m. Steffy." "Okay here is the story" she says. "I got my broken nail fixed but she was all out of blood red and the other red she uses did not match. So we decided they really need to match because I really want to look professional at work." It was all I could do to keep a straight face and not blurt out that she looks like a hooker in a lab coat. "So we decided to use this awesome purple color and next week she will give me a special deal on coloring my hair to match, so I look professional." "Well all righty then." I say. "Listen Liz and I are going to take a break shortly, can you please hold down the fort?" "Okay I will try, but my nails are not completely set up and dry." I just rolled my eyes as I walked to the back.

Liz came into the back room and we decided to go for a walk and talk outside. Liz couldn't resist saying "see ya wouldn't want to be ya" as we walked out. Steffy had a blank look on her face.

Liz and I talk about the fact that we are doing all the work and we barely even notice that Steffy is there. We agree that even when she is here she is not really here. We toss around some ideas about letting Sheryl know, but decide it would not be good to involve Sheryl because we might get separated and not be in the same office. This would cramp our style and ruin our ongoing Scrabble game in the back. We decide to give it a little longer, and then we would take care of Steffy ourselves if she did not shape up.

As we walked back into the lab there are six patients sitting in the lobby and Steffy was just finishing up with a patient.

Mrs. Gourley, who was sitting in the lobby said "thank

goodness you are back. I thought you had quit and I was worried about having to find another lab." "No, we were just on a short break" I let her know. "How long have you been waiting?" "Well about fifteen minutes" she says. This is not good, I think. Mrs. Gourley says "I don't want that weird looking girl drawing my blood. Is she like a zombie person?" I tried not to laugh and tell her that I honestly did not think so.

I quickly register the patients' and Liz and I get them drawn and on their way. I remind Liz that she needed to *check the specimen* when she can.

Literally like one minute later I hear Liz swear and say "damn you Betty." This means Liz has discovered my awesome word on my last turn.

I check the paperwork and just as I had thought Steffy had only drawn one patient the whole time we were gone. As Steffy follows her patient out with the blood in her hand I notice that her patient had a close resemblance to Steffy. "Steffy that young lady looks a lot like you." "Right, and she likes this color on me" Steffy adds. I tell her that we are going to need her to pick up her speed when drawing patients. "Okay I will work on that" she says.

I announce that I am going to lunch. I have to get back before it is time for Liz to leave. I decided to take my lunch to the park to relax in the sun.

I am finishing my lunch and have ten more minutes to enjoy the sun when I notice two old ladies walking towards me. One of them says "well hello there. I was just telling Marge here that you looked like our blood draw person. Do you remember us?" I was thinking of course not, I only draw one hundred people a day. "Yes you look very familiar" I say. "Why are you out here sitting on the grass all alone?" "I am just enjoying some peace and quiet while I eat my lunch," I say.

Most folks would have caught my drift here and maybe excused themselves and said enjoy your lunch. Not these two. "We were in two weeks ago and you did a great job." "Great, glad it went well." "Listen can you look at my arm?" Why, I ask? "Well I was telling Marge we should take our bandages off our arms pretty soon." "Ma'am you can remove your bandages anytime now" I say. "Oh boy look at the time, I must go back to work now." I head to my car with them both watching and waving. I need to find a park further away from the lab.

As I return to the lab and park my car I notice two ambulances in the loading zone. That is always a bad sign. This means I will be getting calls asking for someone to come down and draw some blood. As soon as Liz sees me she starts gathering her things. Boy someone is anxious to leave today. She tells me the processing is all caught up. As she walks out she said "see ya wouldn't want to be ya." I just chuckle. Steffy tells me she is taking a short break. I say fine. I wonder if she ever learned to tell time?

I settle in up front when a cute little old lady walks in. She has her coat on and is carrying an umbrella, her purse and her requisition. She is dressed pretty nice. I greet her and take her lab slip. She is struggling with getting her insurance cards out. She hands me her library card. I tell her I just need your Medicare card, it is the one with red, white and blue. This seems to help a bit. She just needed a CBC, complete blood count. No fasting required. So I go to the door to the lobby and call her back.

She is feeling her way along the wall as we walk back to the draw room, as if she could not see anything. After I draw her blood I asked her if she had a ride? I ask "if there is some-one is here to drive you home? Can I call you a cab?" She says "no honey, I have my car. I am good." I was horrified. This darling little old lady is driving a car alone. My blood runs cold just thinking about her out on the road in her car.

I notice Steffy is pretty quiet. She is sitting up near the front desk in our draw chair looking at a beauty magazine. I sit down at the front desk and ask her if she thought she could close up today? I told her I needed to leave thirty minutes early and stop by the main lab to talk with Sheryl. She says okay. I am a little nervous about this idea but what could happen in thirty minutes right?

The phone rings and Mary down in Urgent Care says she has a draw for us. I send Steffy down because she needs the practice. I head to the back to make sure the processing is caught up. Steffy comes back with the blood. I tell her I am taking off and remind her to shut the machines' down, turn on the answering machine and lock the door at five p.m.

I arrive at the main lab and it is the usual after work nightmare. No parking anywhere. I decide to park along the red curb because I should only be about fifteen minutes and I can see the car from Sheryl's office. As I walk in the front door to the lab Sheryl is at the front counter wheeling and dealing on prices with a cash paying patient. Seriously? She is really good at this. Apparently that is another one of her gimmicks. The patient gets a real low price and a piece of candy.

I head down the hall to her office to wait. As I sit there enjoying a piece of the candy she keeps on her desk I look around her office.

I am looking for her stash of butterfly needles. These smaller needles are used for veins that are especially fragile or small in size. Sheryl has begun rationing them out. I know that they are hidden somewhere in this office.

Liz and I are wondering what in the hell is up with this little game? We have decided if we run out of butterfly needles we will just start sending the hard to draw patients to the main lab and have them ask for Sheryl. This should make our point.

This is all just a small part of why I have been meaning to ask for a raise. Sheryl looks through my file and says "hmmm well I guess we could do twenty five cents more per hour." I say "I was thinking at least fifty." "I tell you what, if I get no complaints for three months then I will up it to fifty cents." I say okay and say goodnight.

I head home in my car thinking I need to buy another lottery ticket. I hate to sound ungrateful, but I am way underpaid. Maybe I should look into delivering pizzas. I think that over for the rest of the ride home.

I remember Sheryl mentioning Dotty would be back tomorrow. Who would have thought I would be excited to have Dotty back with us.

CHAPTER

HERE WE ARE, ANOTHER EXCITING DAY in Whitney Park. "Good morning" I say as I unlock the door to our office. There are only six patients waiting today. Not too bad. I put my stuff in the back and get the lights and machines on while my patients sign in and take a seat. There are two women fighting over the last good magazine.

I call my first patient up to the window. "Mrs. Swanson have you been in to our lab before?" "Yes many times" as she hands me her insurance cards she whispers to me, "listen can you kind of keep quiet and not mention the tests I am having? My nosy neighbor just walked in and it is none of her beeswax what I am having done here." "Oh yes ma'am no problem" I say.

I put her requisition on the counter with a sticky note with Liz's name on it. I keep registering patients.

Liz has just arrived. I see her go to the back room. Looks

like she is *checking the specimen* on our Scrabble board. She walks out buttoning up her lab coat and mentions that I need to *check the specimen* when I get a chance.

I call another patient up. A seemingly nice man Marvin Smith. "Good morning Mr. Smith" I say. "No thank you" he says. As I look at him something is not quite right. Mr. Smith is dressed in jeans, suspenders, a flannel long sleeve shirt and a bright red tie. I notice quite a bit of old dried food on his shirt. He is wearing a baseball cap that says *Here's the Beef Honey.*

I look at his requisition and all he has is a urinalysis. I ask him if he can get me a urine specimen? He says he just went before he left the house. I say okay and give him a good size cup of water to drink and have him take a seat in the waiting room.

I let Liz know what's going on and ask if she can cover the front while I go *check the specimen.* It looks like Liz is ahead by twenty points. I will fix that.

As I finish my turn Dotty walks in. I let her know it is her turn to *check the specimen.* I ask Liz if she has checked on our patient in the waiting room, Mr. Smith. Liz informs me that she gave him a second cup of water. We have a box in the bathroom for the patients to leave their urine samples. I walk out to Mr. Smith holding a cup labeled with his name and hand it to him for when he is ready, and show him where the bathroom is.

About five minutes later I see Mr. Smith head for the bathroom. I walk over to remind him what to do again as I turn on the light for him.

I see Liz is registering several more patients as I walk up to the front desk. I straighten up the waiting room a bit while waiting for Liz to get the patients registered. Well, what a surprise. All the magazines are gone again. I head down the hall to Primary Care to borrow, I mean steal, some of their magazines. I pick up two National Geographic and a couple of Readers' Digest. Very boring, hopefully these will last a week or more. Who would want to steal these right?

Liz is on hold with a doctor's office. The girls in the office know we have the patient standing in front of us but never hurry just the same. I can hear a patient loudly asking Liz why they ordered a pregnancy test when she had a hysterectomy fifteen years ago? Whew, I am so glad it is Liz up front in the chair and not me.

I hear the bathroom door open and can see Mr. Smith heading to the back of the office instead of to the front waiting room. I help get him turned around and headed out the door. As I enter the bathroom I see things are not quite right in there. Mr. Smith has filled the urine cup all the way up to where it is overflowing and has set it on the sink with no lid. I grab some gloves and get the lid on the specimen. It looks like the toilet is undisturbed. I guess by the looks of things he used the sink to finish peeing. Lovely. I clean the sink and dry it off the best I can and take the urine to the processing room.

As I finish and head to the front to call the next patient I hear Liz say "I need some help in here." I walk into the room and her patient has fainted. Her patient is slumped over in the draw chair. I gently pull the lady into a sitting position in the chair so Liz can remove the needle from her arm. Liz bandaged her up and we carry her over onto our extra exam table.

All righty then, Liz can check on her while I register more patients. All of a sudden I realize I have not seen Dotty in a while. What the hell? I go to the back room where I last saw her. There sits Dotty painting her nails at the table while pondering her next move at scrabble. When she sees my face she immediately closes the bottle and heads up front. I say "it is your turn to draw for awhile." I would never have the nerve to do that to my coworkers. I think Liz and I are going to be taking a day off real soon. Lets see Dotty and Steffy run the lab for one day. The thought is scary.

Looks like Liz's patient has recovered and is up to walking out on her own. Dotty is up front registering a patient. I motion for Liz to follow me to processing room. I suggest we take a break and go for a short walk. Liz is ready for that. I tell Dotty we will be right back. I tell Liz about finding Dotty painting her nails. She was laughing so hard I thought she would pee in her pants.

When she recovered we agree it is time for us to take a mental health day. We agree we would go out to the beach for the day. Now we have something to look forward to.

Liz and I agree to look at our schedules and pick a date in the near future. I feel like I should warn our patients which days not to come in but that would get us in trouble. When we walk back into the office I feel better than when I walked out. Amazing what planning time off does for your spirits.

As we walk in Dotty is in the back drawing a patient and both phone lines are ringing. Liz calls a patient back and I answer the phones.

I put both lines on hold then go back to the first line. There is a STAT draw in Urgent Care. I get up and ask Dotty to please go do the STAT draw as soon as she is finished there. She looks mad but does not dare complain.

I answer the second line. Sheryl says "Betty what is going on down there, the phone rang too many times. You guys need to answer that phone by the second or third ring." I think to myself you have got to be kidding, but say "okay will do." I ask if there is anything else? Sheryl asks if we had an old man in there today? She describes Mr. Smith. I explained we had a man who fit that description awhile ago. Sheryl said that he had wandered out of his assisted living facility and they are looking for him.

Sheryl tells me the police are looking for him right now. Great. I wished her well and tell her that I had to go help draw blood. Apparently Mr. Smith is not supposed to walk to the lab. He is supposed to go in a van with the others. I hope I never get old.

I ask Sheryl if she can send a courier for the STAT? She says okay but not sure how long it will take. Dotty just walked in the door with the blood from Urgent Care. She was looking worn out but did not dare complain. I just said "I am going to lunch." I change into shorts and a t shirt and head to the park to hit some tennis balls.

Wow! I must say I always feel better after forty five minutes of hitting tennis balls. This really improves my mood. Unfortunately this usually only lasts for about fifteen minutes after I settle back into the chair in the front office at the out-patient lab.

Actually, right now the lab looks fairly calm. Liz has just *checked the specimen*. She has taken her turn in our ongoing Scrabble game in the back room. She is gathering her things together getting ready to leave. I would love it if it was a nice quiet afternoon.

As I settle in to the seat at the front counter Liz says "see ya wouldn't want to be ya" as she happily walks out.

The phone rings and as I pick up, Sheryl says "Betty you

are just the gal I am looking for." It always concerns me when she starts out this way. "Yes, I was thinking maybe I will send a tech down there next Monday and show you and Liz how to run a few tests."

A tech is a Medical Technologist from our main lab who runs the tests on the blood we draw. "This way we can give Urgent Care a faster turnaround time." "You do remember that we are phlebotomists and not techs right?" I say. "Yes but I think you two can handle this easily." Seriously? We cannot even keep up with drawing the blood I am thinking. Well I guess we will plan on this for next Monday then. Great, I guess we cannot make Monday our beach day.

I ask Dotty if she can come sit at the front desk while I go *check the specimen*. Yippee my turn at scrabble. Liz has just used the Z to score over fifty points. Damn her. Well I have the Q, let me see what kind of damage I can do?

As I walk out I see Dotty has registered three patients. Dotty takes one man to the back to her draw chair and I call another to my draw chair in the front. This patient seemed fairly nice, and not super uptight or afraid. I am just getting started when Dotty walks out and says "I need you to draw the patient in my chair when you are through." She looks a little upset. I say "okay tell him I will be with him in a few minutes."

I finish drawing my patient and Dotty takes the blood to the back to process while I bring her patient over to my chair. I usually draw up front so I can sit on a stool to draw blood. I say hello as I get everything ready. I ask if anything happened a few minutes ago with Dotty? He said "beats me she just got up and walked out." "Well okay" I said.

As I was tying the tourniquet I notice that with me sitting

on the stool I was at eye level with this gentleman. Seems okay to me. Just as I was finished tying the tourniquet and looking for my spot to draw I notice that this patients arm was in very close proximity to my right breast. As he opened his hand after making a fist I noticed his fingers were rubbing against my breast.

Okay, I am thinking surely that was an accident. As the tubes were filling he did it again and gave me a wink. I simply say "listen buddy, keep your fingers still, if you ever do that again I will stick this needle clear through your arm until it comes out the other side. I hope we understand each other."

He had a scared look on his face, like he had never thought that was a possibility. I tape his arm and gave him a huge smile and say "you have a nice day now." He gets up and walks out. Well this job just gets more fun each and every day.

As I take the blood to the processing room Dotty looks at me and says she never wants to draw that guy again. I say that's okay I will draw him. She gives me a confused but grateful look. I tell her how I handled it and she looks horrified. I am finding as I get older I have a lot less patience. Dotty is a bit timid and always surprised if not horrified at how bold I can be. Tomorrow is Friday. Yippee a weekend! I ask Dotty to cover the front while I go to the back to call Liz at home.

I call Liz and learn that she is watching talk shows and eating ice cream. Liz has a husband who works a lot of hours so she gets a little bored.

I tell her the most recent incident regarding my last patient. I wait until she finishes laughing then we agree we will both take a mental health day next Friday and go out to the coast for the day. We seem to agree that the worst day at the beach would be better than the best day at work.

CHAPTER

I HAVE JUST ARRIVED AT THE LAB ready to start a new day. There are six patients waiting. As I walk through Urgent Care to head down the hall John in Urgent Care tells me that we are having a drug rep luncheon today. He says, "take turns coming down for a free lunch and some goodies."

What happens is the drug reps bring lunch along with an assortment of notepads, clipboards, calculators and other goodies all with the name of the current drugs they are trying to push the doctors into prescribing to their patients. They provide a nice lunch for the staff.

Wow, now my mood has picked up considerably. These always are good lunches. He says it is being catered by a local Mexican restaurant. We usually get pens, notepads and other cool stuff.

Last time we went to one of these affairs over at the main lab we got mirrors that we stuck to the side of our computer monitors so we could see our supervisor walking down the hall and heading towards us. Boy what awesome little gadgets those were. They give us plenty of time to get off of a web site we were not supposed to be on or stop playing solitaire and pull up the labs site.

As I open the front door I say my usual "good morning folks, please sign in and have a seat." "Ma'am how long will this take?" a woman asks. "I have a doctors appointment down the hall in twenty minutes. I tell her "you probably should go to your doctors appointment and then stop by on your way out and have your blood drawn." "I am already starving, I don't know if I can fast for that long" she says. "Well let me know what you decide to do" I say.

I call my first patient. "Good morning" I say as she hands me her requisition. Are you fasting? Yes, I have not eaten anything. I did drive thru Starbucks earlier for a Latte though. "You probably need to come back on a morning when you have had nothing but water after dinner the night before" I tell her. Ten hours of fasting is good. "I don't think this Latte is going to make any difference will it?" "Yes, it most likely has sugar in it." "I am sure it will be fine" she says. "Okay, but your results will not be accurate." "Whatever, just draw my blood." "Okay, may I please see your insurance card then you can take a seat. I will call you back shortly." I make a note on her requisition that this patient is fasting except for the Latte, but is insisting on being drawn.

Liz has just arrived, and has taken her turn at our ongoing Scrabble game. She says to me "when you get a chance can you *check the specimen*?" I tell Liz we have a drug rep lunch down the hall. Her eyes perk up.

I register two more patients. I ask Liz if she could take

results down to Primary Care and let them know we have a drug rep lunch starting at noon.

I bring Mrs. Roland around to my draw chair. I check her arms for the best vein while exchanging a few words about it being a beautiful day. "Listen I must warn you, my veins roll" she lets me know. "Oh okay not a problem" I say.

Every other patient tells me their veins roll. As I am labeling the tubes and finishing up with Mrs. Roland Dotty walks in. I ask Dotty if she can start drawing so we can get the waiting room cleared out. The phones are ringing so I answer both lines, putting one on hold. Mrs. Jones is asking if she has to fast? She is struggling to pronounce the names of the tests. So we figure out that yes she needs to fast. I go to the next phone line. It is Sheryl.

She says she needs Dotty to come to the main lab and she will send Steffy down to us. Oh boy what a swell trade. I almost say don't bother, but I keep my mouth shut. I decide to slip into the back room to *check the specimen*. Damn Liz! She just made another thirty point word. I need a whopping word to pull ahead. Okay, now we are almost tied. I leave the room feeling quite happy with myself.

As I walk out Liz says Cedrick is here for his Protime. I look out the window and sure enough there he is peeing on the front of the building. People are just staring as they walk on by.

We have tried to get Mr. Murphy to stop peeing on the building with no success. I pull Mr. Murphy's paperwork and sure enough here he comes, stumbling through the door. Looks like maybe his wife Mary might be gone and he dressed himself. He has on a pair of shorts that are about two sizes too small. I can see now that he forgot underwear and forgot to zip his fly. His t-shirt is too short and his belly is showing. I get out a sticky pad and put Liz's name on the requisition so it appear that he requested her. She has too easy of an afternoon today and we have to share the misery. Dotty and I walk down the hall to see if there is any food out yet. Liz looks very busy with Mr. Murphy. It looks slow down at Urgent Care. That is awesome. Happy Friday to all of us.

Dotty and I manage to snag a couple plates with Guacamole and salsa and we bring some back for Liz. The main food will not be out for another forty five minutes. I also snag a couple of awesome pens and notepads. Dotty said she is heading over to the main lab. I see Mr. Murphy heading out through the lobby, I hold the door open for him and tell him to have a nice day.

Liz comes out and brings Mr. Murphy's blood to the back. I tell her Dotty has just headed to the main lab for the rest of the day and Sheryl was sending Steffy down to help us out for the afternoon. She laughs and wishes me luck.

Liz is slipping into the back room to *check the specimen*. I settle in at the front desk. Liz comes out and says she is done with her turn at Scrabble and heads down to see if the food was out?

Liz comes back with a plate full of Mexican food. So I head down to fill up a plate for myself while she watches the front window. Liz and I actually got to finish our plates of food without any patients coming in. Liz tells me that Bill and Jackie in Urgent Care were looking quite chummy in the break room where the food is. I said, "oh you have no idea." So I proceed to tell her about me finding them in the shower. This of course brings a big laugh.

We talk a little more about our mental health day to the

beach coming up on Friday. Sometimes everyone needs a mental health day, but particularly if you work in this field. It is difficult to work with the public in general, however working in the medical field is even tougher because you have to get physically close to the patient to draw their blood.

We also have to deal with patients hangups and fears. A lot of people have had bad experiences with shots as children and have never been able to move past it. Some are literally terrified of needles. They do not realize we are just barely inserting the needle under the skin into the vein. After dealing with these issues day in and day out it really helps our mental health to have breaks periodically.

It is almost one p.m. and here comes Steffy through the door. She looks a little rushed and things are falling out of her purse. Oh my she has on new fake nails that are an interesting shade of purple. She also has a new hairdo that matches her nails. She is quite proud that her hair and nails match. I am wondering how many nails will have to fall off before she realizes having super long claw-like nails does not work when you are a phlebotomist. I am thinking the first time she injures a patient with the nails that will be the end it.

Liz is just now walking out of the back room after *checking the specimen.*

I see her do a double take when she sees Steffy standing there with purple hair. Being located in California does not help. People who live in California in general are accustomed to an anything goes attitude. I think management is afraid of saying anything to her for fear of a lawsuit. So we make general conversation with Steffy about what she has been up to. All of a sudden Liz says "well time for me to go home." I dread those words. Liz walks out the door saying "see ya wouldn't want to be ya."

I settle in to my seat in the front office and the phone rings. I answer and it is Sheryl. She tells me the medical technologist will be at our office on Monday to show Liz and I how to run a few easy common tests that are frequently ordered by Urgent Care, like a rapid strep test which detects strep throat, a pregnancy test, and a couple others.

If they can have us run a few tests right here in Whitney Park it will make the Urgent Care and Primary Care offices happy and will save SuperLab time and money. SuperLab will not have to pay a medical technologist to do it and of course they make more money than phlebotomists.

I decide to have Steffy work the front desk registering patients and I will draw the blood, so hopefully we will not get too backed up. I tell her I am going in the back to *check the specimen*. As I walk towards the back I hear an old lady asking Steffy if she is dressed up for Halloween, and what she is dressing up as? I just snicker to myself. Apparently she was not even slightly embarrassed by the question or her appearance.

Steffy is fairly young and seems to have no idea how to dress professionally. Then I hear the old lady ask her how can she pick anything up or do anything with those long nails? I have to say I am really getting a kick out of listening to Steffy try and deal with this old lady and her questions.

I tell Steffy I will be right back and that I am going to go get the mail. This should be great fun letting her open all the stool cards in the mail.

The mailbox is out in front of the building. As I am heading back inside I grab four magazines from the table in the lobby of Urgent Care.

I walk in to the lab and see there are three patients waiting and Steffy is not yet drawing any blood. So I grab my lab coat and call the first patient. Marge Johnson, a pretty nice lady. I finally figure out that she is the wife of Larry Johnson. He is one of our newer patients.

Actually he was a pain in the ass. She is a saint to put up with him. He was the one who kept me on the phone for what seemed like forever trying to get directions. I almost swallowed my gum when Mrs. Johnson asked me what was up with Steffy out front and her purple hair? I have to be careful what I say because I have been getting too many calls from Sheryl lately. So I basically just let her vent and I agreed it was very interesting and colorful.

As I walk her blood to the back to get it processed I notice Steffy is drawing blood from another patient. I decide to work on processing and let her draw the blood. When she finishes these two draws I will let her open the mail. Just thinking about that makes me laugh out loud.

I start the centrifuge and head out to the front desk. Looks like Steffy is starting to draw her last patient. Honestly, I think if she was going any slower she would be going in reverse. I see some results printing so I pull them off and take them down the hall to Primary Care. Woo hoo! Only one more hour until we close.

As I walk back in from delivering the results I see Steffy is on the phone in the back with the on again off again boyfriend. I think they are off again right now. With all the patience I could muster I go to the back and ask nicely for her to come up front as soon as possible.

As Steffy comes up front I ask her if she is familiar with the occult blood cards or stool cards? She thinks she has heard of them but doesn't know how to give a patient instructions on how to collect them and does not know what to do with the ones we get in the mail.

So as Steffy starts opening the mail I show her which things we throw out, which ones go to Sheryl and how to handle the stool cards. Steffy starts to open the stool cards and I remind her to check and make sure the patient's name is on them. As she opens the first card she pulls it out and gets poop all over her hands. I almost wet my pants laughing.

Steffy looks absolutely horrified and drops the card on the floor and runs to the bathroom. She has been in there for twenty minutes now washing her hands. Okay, so miss Steffy is back from her hand washing and is wearing gloves.

I am registering a patient while she cleans the floor and rebags the stool cards. Seriously, you just cannot believe how much fun we have in the outpatient lab!

I call my patient back while Steffy cleans up the poop and opens the remaining cards. The patient kind of looks at her but does not say much except "it smells kind of yucky in here."

Finally our day is coming to a close, so we are getting things ready for the courier. Just as I think this is about to end here comes a young mother with a baby. Steffy is livid. I am thinking what are you mad about? I'm the one who has to draw the blood. She has no idea how to draw a baby. Great, just what I want to do is draw a baby and deal with a crying mother ten minutes before we close.

When this happens it is a given that we both will be working thirty minutes longer and the courier will have to wait for the blood. I would send her to the main lab but there is nobody there at this hour that knows how to draw a baby.

To draw blood from a baby you really have to have at least

ten years experience and you have to know how to draw with a syringe. Apparently they are no longer teaching these young people how to draw with a syringe. Babies and the elderly are similar in that respect. To do a great job and leave very little bruising it is necessary to use a syringe. When you draw blood with a butterfly needle attached to the vacutainer which is the way the new people do every draw it creates a vacuum. It pulls the blood out very quickly collapsing the patient's vein if they have a tiny vein. When you use a syringe the phlebotomist can control how fast the blood comes out. It is amazing what a difference this makes.

I ask Steffy to lock the front door and join us in the back. She will need to hold the baby in a certain position to keep the baby from moving, while I draw the blood. The mothers' are seldom able to hold the baby. They usually are crying and quite upset, unless they are a fellow phlebotomist or nurse themselves. I think this is Steffy's' first time assisting with a baby. She has to learn some time.

Our courier is now waiting in the processing room for the specimen, which is good because it is a STAT which means the doctor wants the results right away. I draw the blood using a syringe and get the blood into special small tubes that require less blood. I leave Steffy to hold pressure on the baby's arm and then put a little bandage on. I get the blood for the courier and start turning off the machines and lights. The mother has composed herself and we usher her out and we are done with this day.

CHAPTER

OH NO, IS IT MONDAY ALREADY? I keep pushing the snooze button hoping it is a dream, and not a work day yet. Unfortunately it is a work day, and if I want to have a place to live I must get myself up out of bed and get into the shower. As I am washing my hair I take extra care to make sure the cream rinse is all out. My last incident with forgetting to rinse the cream rinse out and not noticing until I was on the way to work is still fresh in my mind. I think today is definitely coffee and donuts day.

As I am driving to work it occurs to me that I could probably make the same amount of money working in a donut shop, without any exposure to hepatitis C or HIV. The risks of sticking myself with a dirty needle are very real. The way I get through it is to just be as careful as possible and forget it. Yes, this is a high risk job.

Phlebotomists must have their blood drawn and checked on a regular basis, then again if you stick yourself with a needle, to make sure you have not contracted anything.

I contemplate a change in jobs as I drive to work munching on my donuts and drinking my coffee. My mother wanted me to follow in her footsteps and go into the nursing field. I knew early on that I did not have enough patience to be a nurse. I can imagine my mother's face if she found out I had quit my job as a phlebotomist to work in a donut shoppe.

My mother always gets embarrassed when I compliment strangers on their great veins. I actually would miss drawing blood if I left the field. I am a true vampire. I love watching the blood flow into the tubes. I do not tell most people this because it freaks them out. My problem is that I run out of patience with certain patients. Apparently the phlebotomy field has a high rate of burn out. Go figure!

"Well happy Monday" I say to myself as I climb out of my car at Whitney Park Health Center.

As I head down the hall to unlock the door I see an interesting situation. Two elderly male patients, a scooter and some commotion. Apparently the two elderly gentleman are buddies and were both riding on one scooter. While the smaller gentleman was on the bigger gentleman's lap he hit the wrong button on the scooter and they crashed into the glass next to the front door to the lab.

Now they are both off the scooter taking punches at each other and swearing at each other. I hear one say "now what am I supposed to tell my wife?" I see the glass is cracked and I will now have to call Sheryl with more good news. I get everyone moved back and the fight broken up so I can open the door. I am so excited for Fridays trip to the beach.

It looks like we have about ten patients already waiting. I will start registering patients and then call Sheryl while Liz draws the patients. I ask the two gentlemen with the scooter to please leave the scooter outside. They are still fighting about which one hit the wrong button causing the scooter to hit the window.

I call my first patient up to the window. "Good morning Mr. Kennedy, how are you today?" I say. "Good morning" he says. I ask if he is fasting? "I just had eggs and toast" he says. "Sir you are going to have to come back another day. You must be fasting for these tests." You can have dinner the night before and then just have water all evening and in the morning until we draw your blood. "Well how am I going to do that?" he says. "My wife makes popcorn with butter every night while we watch TV. I cannot sit there while she has popcorn and not eat any."

"Sir, you will have to figure this out on your own, I have to call the next patient as we have lots of people waiting." He is mumbling as he waddles out the door. I call my next patient.

Liz has just arrived. "Good morning Mr. Owens, how are you today?" I ask if he is fasting? "Yes, and I am starving." "Okay great if you will have a seat someone will call you back shortly." I call the next patient.

I see Mrs. Weinstein has just walked in and has one of those cooler type bags. Apparently she has brought food. As she approaches the window to sign in on the clipboard she asks how long the wait is. I say "about forty five minutes." She gives a big sigh and says "I hope I don't faint." I reply "I hope not, can you take a seat please." She looks for a seat and then starts whining because there are no magazines left.

I go on to the next patient. The sooner we get them drawn, the sooner we can work on other things. I am dread-ing calling Sheryl.

I register the rest of the patients and start drawing blood. Liz has been drawing blood steadily and the room is slowly emptying out. There is a line for the bathroom. It is very common for patients to have to leave a urine specimen.

As the last patient goes back to be drawn with Liz I decide to go to the back and *check the specimen* before calling Sheryl. It is my turn in our ongoing Scrabble game. I walk out and ask Liz if she can *check the specimen* when she gets a chance?

I tell Liz I need to call Sheryl about the front window. She snickers and says "I noticed there was a large crack in the front window." So I settle down in the back and dial Sheryl and leave her a message telling her we had a little incident down here and I need to speak to her as soon as possible. I know she is going to be upset. Anything that costs the lab more money makes her mad. I mean honestly you would think it was coming straight out of her paycheck by the way she acts.

I see Liz is registering a few more people, so I pull the results off the printer and take them down the hall to Primary Care and see if I can steal some magazines for the waiting room while I am at it.

When I get back I drop some more magazines in the waiting room as I walk in. Liz says "Sheryl called for you." I call the main lab and ask for Sheryl. I get put on hold. Sheryl comes on the line. "Betty what's going on?" "Well Sheryl we had a little incident down here this morning." "What happened?" says Sheryl. I relate the whole story about the two old men on the scooter and Sheryl says she will send somebody down to fix the glass.

Before we hang up Sheryl adds "Betty, I think you need to come down to the main lab for a while. I will send Steffy down to help out in your place. I think you need a change of pace. So next week I want you to come to the main lab at seven a.m." I say goodbye and hang up.

Well, it looks like Liz and I taking our mental health day and going to the beach this Friday is perfect timing. Wait till I tell her about this. When I get off the phone with Sheryl I tell Liz quietly what Sheryl said. Liz is not happy because this means she will be stuck working with Dotty and Steffy.

Liz says "the medical technologist is on their way." Great, Dotty will be doing all the registering and drawing of the blood while Liz and I learn how to run a few tests in the back room. I walk down to the Urgent Care to steal a cup of coffee from the pot. I need to be wide awake for our instruction.

I sit down to enjoy my coffee before the tech gets here. Dotty is here and has agreed to work the front desk. Liz walks by me headed to the processing room. I let her know that it is her turn to *check the specimen*." At this point the processing is all caught up and Dotty is sitting at the front desk as Liz and I head to the back to learn how to run a few tests. An hour later I feel like management is definitely taking advantage of us. Honestly I am wondering if this is even legal. Liz and I are phlebotomists, not medical technologists.

Well, I need this job so I guess I will keep my mouth shut and do what I am told. I sit at the front counter while Liz and Dotty both take breaks before I go to lunch.

The phone is ringing. I answer it and it is a young woman wanting to know if we make house calls? I ask her to repeat herself because I am thinking I must have heard her wrong. No I heard her right. She goes on to tell me about her very important job answering phones for an answering service and she cannot find time to get her blood drawn. I give her the address and phone number to our main lab, and explain they are open until six p.m. and on Saturdays. I wish her the best and hang up. Unbelievable!

I am feeling burned out and annoyed today. That probably has something to do with the fact that I had to wade through motorcycle parts spread all over the living room floor to get to the bathroom this morning.

My son Jared is home sick from school with Mono and is rather bored. So he took his dirt bikes' engine apart to rebuild it or something like that. Geez I wish I was paying more attention last night when he apparently mentioned his plan. He is supposed to be doing school work, which I had to go get on my lunch hour several times, and then I have to return it to his teachers when it is completed. I feel like there is a tattoo on my forehead labeled SLAVE.

I am not sure how I feel about working at the main lab for awhile. Well, it's not like Sheryl gave me a choice. At least I have Friday to look forward to.

Okay Liz and Dotty are both back from their breaks which means I can go to lunch. Yippee. I am going to just relax in the sun and grab a sandwich at Port O Subs. I get my sandwich and just sit in my car in the sun at a park. Boy the sun feels so good, I wish I could stay here all day. I think I deserve an extra fifteen minutes here due to all the fifteen minute breaks I never get.

As I am driving back to the lab I am wishing that I could switch hours with Liz but I need full time. It is not cheap raising a teenage boy. I walk into the lab and see Liz gathering her stuff as she is getting ready to leave for the day.

When I return from lunch I see that Dotty has several registered patients waiting while she is registering more patients, all who are waiting to have their blood drawn. I put my stuff down and get my lab coat on and get ready to call the next patient.

Liz comes out of the break room and says "when you get a chance can you *check the specimen?*" I can only imagine what kind of fifty point word she made in our ongoing Scrabble game. As I call a patient back Liz smiles and says "see ya wouldn't want to be ya" as she walks out the door.

I call Judy Swanson back. I make light conversation as we head to my draw chair. This was actually an easy draw as we say. No fear of needles and no whining about anything. Why can't they all be like this. I tape her arm and wish her a good rest of her day.

As I walk past the desk to the processing room with the blood I just drew I hear Dotty speaking to someone on the phone. It appears that they are angry about something. I motion for her to put them on hold. So she does and I ask what is going on? She says there is a man on the line who says he is supposed to collect a semen analysis and is not happy because we do not have any dirty magazines here at the lab for him to look at. He wants to know if he can bring his wife with him to help him collect the sample? I tell Dotty to refer him to the main lab. It is for fertilization and needs to be kept at body temperature. She gives him the news and he is not happy.

I pulled some new results off the printer and head down the hall to Primary Care to deliver them. I figure I can see about picking up maybe two more magazines for our waiting room.

Two more hours until quitting time! Not that I am watching the clock or anything. When I walk back into the lab Dotty said Sheryl called and said Steffy was coming down here for the rest of the week. "Wonderful, just wonderful" I say.

The phone rings and Urgent Care says we are bringing samples to you. We need you to run monospot and HCG tests. The monospot is to check to see if the patient has mononucleosis, and the HCG is a pregnancy test.

This day just keeps getting better and better. This will be my first time running these tests after being shown only once. It just blows my mind what this lab will do to save a dime. Plus, the doctor and the patient are relying on these results being accurate. The doctor might prescribe medication based on the result I turn out.

I informed Dotty that I have to run a couple of tests, so she will have to register the patients and draw the blood. No sooner do I start the tests in the back and Dotty comes into the room letting me know that our baby for the thyroid test is here to be drawn. I tell Dotty that she is going to have to ask the mother to bring the baby back tomorrow morning or take the baby to the main Lab. It takes two people to draw a baby, one to hold the baby so it does not move and another to draw. I also remind Dotty that whatever you do, do not let the mother hear you refer to her baby as "The Thyroid Baby."

Is it Friday yet?

Honestly I think Sheryl has lost her mind moving me to the main lab. There is certainly no way Dotty and Steffy can run this office by themselves after Liz leaves. "Oh well, the good news is that there is a taco place around the corner that has great food." I can't wait to see how this plays out. Liz will call me with all the sordid details. The main lab might just be a lot of fun. Last time I worked in the main lab there were all kinds of things happening.

Well I am looking forward to the beach on Friday.

CHAPTER

HERE WE GO AGAIN. Another day beginning here in Whitney Park. As I walk down the hall I see there are only four people waiting outside the door. I am so happy. "Good morning" I say as I open the door and turn the lights on. I tell the patients to please sign in and that I will be right with them. I get machines turned on, my lab coat on, my purse in a drawer and we are ready to begin our day. I guess I am looking for Steffy to arrive somewhere around nine a.m.

I call my first patient. "Good morning Mrs. Brown, how are you today?" "Well honey I tell you I am just not very happy. Ever since my Marty retired I do not have a moments peace. I am not sure what I am going to do? It appeared that he could not hear me so we got him hearing aids. Two days ago I caught him red handed turning his hearing aids off. I am not meaning to nag him but all he does is cook and make messes. He has to find something to do during the day to give me a break."

Okay, way more information than I really need.

"I'm sorry to unload on you dear. Do you have a husband?" "No I am divorced" I tell her. "Oh you are so lucky" she says. I just smile and ask her if she was fasting? I call her back to the draw chair as the story continues. I finish drawing her blood and wished her well.

As I am walking to the back with her blood I see Liz come in the door. Awesome! I say good morning and headed into the back to *check the specimen*. Liz agrees to register some more patients. Five minutes later I walk out of the break room and ask Liz if she could please *check the specimen* when she has a chance? We both love this scrabble game. It really breaks up the day and gives us a little fun. I will miss that when I am at the main lab. I see Liz has registered some patients so I call the next patient back.

"Good morning Mr. Scott. How are you?" I say as he settles into my draw chair. "Pretty good young lady" he says. I am checking his arms for the best vein. I finish drawing his blood and give him a urine cup. I explain to him how to do it and where to put it in the bathroom. Liz has taken a patient into her room and we are briefly caught up.

Liz and I set a time to meet for our mental health day on Friday. I see Steffy come in the door and head to the back to put her stuff away. We all say hello. I tell Liz that I am going to show Steffy how to order supplies. Liz starts laughing and says "oh boy." Liz agrees to hold down the fort in the front while I work with Steffy on how to order supplies. After giving Steffy instructions I leave her alone to complete the order. Sheryl told me to quit holding her hand and doing everything for her.

CHAPTER

I AM TRYING TO GET UP and into the shower to get to work. You really cannot be late because the people are waiting at the door before eight a.m. Each one thinks for sure they will faint or die because they have had nothing to eat since dinner the night before, and are two hours late on having their breakfast. Same story every morning.

I am off to work. I am going to drive through McDonald's and get an Egg McMuffin with sausage and a coffee. I am thinking the sooner I die, the sooner I am done with this job.

I run into the liquor store and buy another Lottery ticket. Okay I am finally at work with five minutes to spare. If you are late you never hear the end of it, plus they call the main lab complaining and Sheryl knows you were late.

As I arrive and walk down the hall to open the door to the lab I can see I have about seven patients waiting. I say my usual good morning as I open the door. I see a little old lady has dropped her purse as she walked in and several things have fallen all over the floor. People are stepping around her in a hurry to get to the front of the line.

I walk to the back room, and get the lights and machines on and get my lab coat on. I am heading for the front desk to start drawing blood. I am glad I had some coffee. It is hard to be ready to draw blood the second you walk in the door.

I call Marilyn Smith up to the window. She seems pleasant. I get her insurance info and make sure she is fasting. I bring her back while the rest of the people finish signing in. I see Liz has arrived. Now the line will start moving.

Liz asks if I ordered any more lavender tubes? I remind her that I showed Steffy how to order supplies, so I believe they have been ordered. I will double check with Steffy when she gets here. She has no certain time she arrives. Usually when the spirit moves her!

I make conversation with Marilyn as I get her blood drawn. I give her a urine cup and instructions on how to collect it and where to leave it in the bathroom.

I have started telling the patients not to fill the cup all the way up to the top and to make sure the lid is on tight. I write the patient's name on the cup and their date of birth so we can clearly read it. I see Liz drawing blood so I tell her I am going to *check the specimen* in the back. Woo hoo! I did a spectacular word. Boy will Liz be upset. Forty six points in one turn.

As I am getting ready to leave the break room Steffy walks in. She looks a bit different today. I am trying to figure out what is different without staring at her. Oh, she has on purple scrubs and has put purple laces in her athletic shoes. She also has purple hair and purple nails all to match. I mention to her that there is a lot of purple. "Well I think I look more professional if everything matches" she tells me. I just nod my head up and down.

"Oh my, sometimes it is hard not to laugh." I have noticed the patients seem to either love her look or hate it. Patients over fifty generally do not care for it and some of them refuse to let her draw their blood.

While Liz is drawing blood I ask Steffy where she put the order form for the supply order she did yesterday? She is digging through her purse. I say "Steffy, let's pick a spot here in the front office to put all order forms." I show her where to put the order forms and how to check stuff off on the form when we get the supplies. I give her a copy of our last order and show her where we keep the file for past orders.

I call Steffy over and ask if she can pull the results off the printer and lets get them down to Urgent Care. I have to make sure she knows how to do it because it will be up to her or Dotty on Friday. I try not to laugh just thinking about it. Steffy heads out the door to deliver the results.

I see Liz has several people registered so I call a patient back to get their blood drawn. Carmen has been in before. A very sweet lady. I make general conversation asking her how she is doing? I can't help but notice that she is really dressed up pretty nice. I have never seen anybody dress that nice for lab work. I am also noticing that she has on a lot of perfume. I am starting to sneeze.

This is very common with elderly women. Many have lost their sense of smell entirely. Others put perfume on then maybe some make up, and after the makeup they put on more perfume because they forgot they already put some on.

The longer I do this job the more I realize that I do not want to live to be super old. She tells me she is going shopping for food for Christmas dinner. We just started the month of June. I just say "okay have fun." I finish up and hold pressure on her arm a little longer so she doesn't get any blood on her nice outfit. As I am walking to the processing room I notice that I need to get some blood spinning in the centrifuge. The tubes of blood have to be balanced out.

We have some tubes filled with water at various levels. You hold a tube of blood up and pick a tube of water that is filled up to nearly the same level as the blood. Then you put them in a slot of the centrifuge opposite one another.

Shoot, I better have Steffy load this so she gets the hang of it. If the tubes are not balanced right the centrifuge sounds like a rocket being launched. Scares the patients and can break the tube. If that should happen you have to clean up all the blood and call the patient back to be redrawn. Then you have to answer questions about what happened and apologize for screwing it up. Not pleasant.

I see our courier has arrived with supplies. I ask Liz if she can *check the specimen* when she gets a chance. I tell Liz that I will let Steffy unpack and put away the supplies. We both know that this is important if she and I are going to take regular mental health days.

I tell Steffy that I will keep the processing going and watch the front while she takes care of the supplies. I keep processing. Well about fifteen minutes later Steffy appears in the doorway looking stressed. She says "umm, can you help me? There is a problem with the butterfly needles." I am starting to get concerned. What could possibly be wrong with the butterfly needles?

As I walk out to where we keep our supplies I see there are boxes everywhere. I ask her if she asked the courier any questions about all these boxes? Apparently she did not and the courier is now gone. I ask Steffy to show me the order form? I look at her order form and compare it to our last order.

I almost did not see it. It looks like she has too many zero's on the order sheet. Now it looks like we have been sent like sixty thousand twenty three gauge butterfly needles for one week's use.

I am really irritated at this point and decide to call supplies over at the main lab. "Hi Ken this is Betty down in Whitney Park." "Hi there what can I do for you?" he says. I said, "Ken we have too many butterfly needles down here. What happened?" He tells me that he has no idea. He looks at his copy of the order form and says "oh, looks like somebody ordered a ridiculous amount of butterfly needles. Ha ha ha." I said "listen Ken are you meaning to tell me that you guys do not check the order and nobody questioned that sixty thousand butterfly needles for one week was too many? Silence. "Uh ya, nobody caught it." "Can we send them back with the courier?" "Let me ask, hang on. Betty, the supervisor says just keep them." "Ken, where are we supposed to put sixty thousand butterflies in this office?" "I'm not sure, I need to get the other line, anything else?" "No, thanks Ken" I say and hang up.

Meanwhile Liz walks out of the break room from *checking the specimen*. She just finished her turn at Scrabble and most likely did a huge fifty point word.

"What's up with all the needles everywhere?" Liz asks. Apparently there was a mistake on our order form and nobody in supplies thought to question sending sixty thousand butterflies down here for us to use in one week. Liz just rolls her eyes and laughs. So Steffy starts putting them away in the normal cupboard and then continues putting them anywhere there is a slight hole in any closet.

I am feeling very disgusted and burned out. I excuse myself to *check the specimen.* As I get to the Scrabble game I see Liz has done another big word. I decide to settle in back here and not leave this room until I come up with a major word.

When I walk out of the break room there are several requisitions on the counter. I see the top one has my name on it. As I call the patient back I don't recognize this patient so Liz most likely has put my name on a difficult patient as if they requested me. This is part of a game we play with each other every day. One of the creative ways we attempt to make the day more fun. If a patient is difficult to deal with at the front counter it is usually worse when you bring them back to draw their blood. Sometimes it helps for them to have a different person in the back. Unfortunately sometimes it makes no difference at all.

I see that Steffy is actually drawing blood from a patient in her room. I go to the door and call Mrs. Stevens back. I make small talk asking her how she is doing on this fine day? Big mistake. As soon as she starts speaking I realize why Liz handed her off to me.

"Well Honey I honestly don't know what's wrong with me? Can you please tell me what's wrong with me? I am not sleeping well and I am tired in the mornings. I ask "what did your doctor say?" "Nothing, he never tells me anything. Maybe I am dying? Do you think I have cancer?" Being a phlebotomist requires us keeping a perfect poker face no matter what the patient says or asks.

We must keep a blank face at all times. When we look at the requisition we can usually tell by the tests ordered what the doctor is looking for. We must never give any indication that we know anything. "Well let's see about getting your blood drawn so we can get these results to your doctor." "Is this going to hurt a lot?" she asks. "No Ma'am I do not believe it will hurt a lot. Maybe just a little." I tell her. "Can you tell me before you put the needle in, I don't want to look." "Okay just close your eyes" I said. "Oh my God, why are you drawing so many tubes?" "Well we just need to draw all the right tubes for the tests ordered. Okay we are all done, can you hold pressure for me on your arm?" I am labeling the tubes, as Liz walks by and sticks her head in the door smiling. Damn her! She handed this lady off to me on purpose.

My special patient walks out and I see several patients waiting. I announce that it is time for me to go to lunch. Liz gives me a look. I think I need to go hit some tennis balls today.

As I am gathering my shorts and t shirt, and heading to the bathroom both of the phones are ringing. Steffy has gone on a break so I tell Liz I will grab line two if she gets line one. "SuperLab may I help you?" "Uh yes I need to get some lab work done." Okay I give the address. "What are these tests for?" I ask. "Did you ask your doctor?" "No I am kind of afraid of him if you know what I mean?"

"Ma'am can you hold for just a moment?" I say. "Liz it's for you" I say as I head to the bathroom to change. I am chuckling to myself.

Okay off to the park I go. Boy it is down right beautiful today. Maybe I should find a job working outdoors. I check my watch so I know how much time I have. I will have to forgo the shower as I need to stop and grab a sandwich to eat at the desk. It would really suck if I had to actually eat my lunch on my lunch break. I love being able to eat at the front desk in between patients.

Wow there is nobody at the park, great news for me. Last thing I need is for one of the patients seeing me falling all over myself trying to hit tennis balls at the park.

I feel much better after thirty minutes of hitting tennis balls. I am going to grab a sandwich and head back to the lab.

As I walk in the door a sweaty mess there are five patients waiting and Steffy is registering additional patients. I don't see Liz. This feels weird my being in shorts and a t shirt carrying my scrubs. The patients are watching me. Not sure if they are trying to figure out who I am or what I am doing here. I walk into the bathroom and wipe myself off with water and get my scrubs back on and try to get myself back into professional mode. I walk into the break room to stash my shorts and t shirt.

There sits Liz staring off into space.

She says "oh your back. I needed a break." I tell her to just hang out in here for fifteen minutes and it will be time for her to go. I walk out and get my lab coat on and call a patient.

I call John Wilson back. "Hello Mr. Wilson" I say. "How are you?" "Well I tell you honey if I was any better I couldn't stand it" he says. "Well that's nice to hear" I say. He continues "well how's your day going?" I say "not too bad, but it's early." He laughs. I am thinking well isn't this nice. A normal patient! So I draw his blood and we chat for a few minutes while I hold pressure on his arm and taped it up. I look at his information. He was only sixty five but I think he was a bit too old for me. Too bad. "Well listen you have a nice rest of your day" I say as he gets up out of the draw chair.

"Well honey, maybe if you went out with me my day would be even better." "Hmm that's an interesting proposition" I say. This is a bit awkward. "What do you do in your spare time Mr. Wilson?" "Call me John" he says. "Okay John it is." "Well I play golf, go out to eat, go boating, and fondle women. Not necessarily in that order." At this point I am unsure what to do so I hold out my hand and say "nice meeting you, but I must keep drawing patients right now." "Okay" he says as he hands me his phone number. I tuck it in my bra and head out to see what's going on out front? Liz is heading out the door but makes sure to say "see ya wouldn't want to be ya." I laugh.

CHAPTER

TODAY IS GOING TO BE A GOOD DAY. The worst day at the beach is better than the best day at work. Liz is coming over and we will take my car out to the coast.

I cannot believe I am awake before the alarm goes off! Okay I make my call to the lab saying I am sick and jump in the shower. I wonder if Liz has called yet? I wonder who will be running the lab today? We have decided to meet at ten a.m. and grab sandwiches and drinks on our way out to the coast. I feel better already as we head out to the coast. Why we never thought of an occasional mental health day before I will never know. So we arrive and get our chairs set up and settle in for the day. Awwwww the ocean breeze is awesome.

As Liz and I are walking along the shore it hits me. I ask Liz "do you have any idea who is running the lab today?" She says "no but I will call and see who answers." "Okay cool," I reply. So as we walk along the beach Liz dials the lab. Steffy answers and immediately puts her on hold. Sounds like some-one is really earning her money today! Liz hangs up and we both start laughing.

After we get back to our chairs we chat a little and just en-joyed the salt air and sun. After awhile I dial the labs number to see who was working with Steffy? The phone rings six times then went to the machine. We both laugh some more. As we were collecting shells, an awesome fun game to play came to my mind. I said to Liz "what if we kept them even busier?" Liz looked puzzled. I explained that we could disguise our voices and call every couple hours with a question about a difficult lab test that they have never heard of.

Liz really perked up at the idea of this fun game, and we immediately started thinking about all the tests we know. So we wait for an hour and then we decide it is time for another call to our brilliant coworkers.

Liz dials and disguises her voice the best she can. Steffy answers and Liz pretends to be a patient asking "how to do a fecal fat quantitative test?" This is a stool test. Silence on the other end of the line. Umm ma'am can you hold please while I check into that test? We chuckle while she has us on hold. Approximately fifteen minutes later Steffy comes back on the line and does her best to explain to Liz that she has to collect all her stools for seventy two hours in a can. She thinks that she has to order a can and have a courier bring it, but she is not sure.

She puts Liz on hold again while she finds out if she has any cans? Just the thought of her looking in every supply area to see if she has any cans makes us laugh. Next I hear Liz ask "Um how exactly do I collect this?" Steffy does not under-stand what she means so Liz elaborates asking how to complete this test? She then asks Liz to hold please.

We are pretty sure she had to call Sheryl at the main office, which will remind Sheryl of how lucky she is to have Liz and Betty. Finally Steffy comes back on the line and explains that you collect the stool right into the can that the lab provides. Liz asks "what do I do with the can when I am not using it?" "Ummmm what do you mean?" says Steffy. Liz sighs as she rephrases the question. "Do I just leave it on the counter or what?" "Can you hold please?" Steffy says. Ten minutes later Steffy comes back on the line telling Liz it needs to be refrigerated. Liz thanks her in her best sweet fake voice. Liz hangs up the phone and sighs.

We enjoy our sandwiches and Liz enjoys a beer. We both look at each other and Liz says "why didn't we ever think to do this before?" "We never had a Steffy working with us before" I say.

After about an hour and a half I disguise my voice and place the call. I get Dotty. I disguise my voice and ask a few questions about a mycology (fungus) culture. "Ma'am can you please hold for a moment while I check into this" says Dotty. "Okay sure" I say.

She comes back with a little information. I then ask "how long does this take?" "Oh can you please hold while I check?" "Alright I guess so" I say. This is really cracking me up because I know a fungal culture takes much longer than other cultures. As she comes back on the line with the information I can hear all kinds of commotion in the background. She says she has to go now. I can only imagine what is going on there in the office. I thank her for her help.

Whew, it's nap time! Liz and I have been working too hard. We close our eyes to rest after laughing hysterically. By now we are feeling really happy. As we head to the water we decide Liz will make one more phone call and then we will relax. Boy I feel like a new person. This day has done me a world of good. Next week I have to work at the main lab. It should not take more than a week or two before Sheryl moves me back. I already feel sorry for Liz, working with Steffy and Dotty.

I have to look up at the sky to keep from laughing out loud as Liz dials the lab for the last time. Hard not to laugh as Liz is spelling the test she cannot pronounce. We have decided to ask whoever answers how to collect a clostridium difficile or C Diff for short.

This time it is Dotty who answers the phone. This is another stool test with very specific requirements and we felt pretty certain neither one of them would be able to answer the questions without researching or calling Sheryl. I laugh as it occurs to me that Liz and I are still training them without even being there. So Dotty thinks she has heard of this test but she has not heard of it for awhile and needs to check on it. Liz is on hold while reading a book. I think it is much funnier when Steffy answers.

Dotty is back on the line telling Liz how to collect her stools in a clean dry container that the lab will give her. I am seriously laughing as Liz says "so what do I do with the stool sample after that?" Dotty says "what do you mean?" Liz asks if she just leaves it on the counter or what? "Oh I forgot to check" says Dotty. Hold please. Finally Dotty comes back on the line and says "you need to refrigerate the stools and then bring into the lab." Bingo, just the answer we were waiting for.

Alright this has been thoroughly entertaining but it is time for us to rest some more. We could have made her elaborate and say within how many hours, but decide we will save that for when we get Steffy on the line. It is a beautiful day at the beach.

This has been a real fun day at the beach. Hopefully I will be up to working at the main lab on Monday. I have not worked there in awhile.

One thing I do like about the main lab is all the phlebotomist has to do is draw the blood or look tests up to see what color tubes we need to draw. There are lots more patients though, which means different types of tests also. There are front office girls who register the patients. There are always at least ten patients waiting in line when the office opens at seven a.m. Most of the patients are fasting and cranky because they are two hours past their normal breakfast time. They seriously think they will pass out from not eating and having blood drawn.

CHAPTER

MONDAY MORNING AT THE MAIN LAB and there is a whole line of patients extending out the door and around the corner. The main lab is located right inside the door, as you walk into an atrium area with beautiful plants and about twenty four medical offices here in Misty, California. I put my things away and head to the back to borrow a lab coat. Mine are all in Whitney Park. I forgot how nice it is to have about ten minutes to gather your thoughts while the front office girls get the patients registered.

Apparently I will be drawing in the hallway in the second draw chair. It is located next to the bathroom and drinking fountain. I am noticing a rack in the hallway. Apparently over here at this lab we instruct the patients to pour their urine from the cup into a tube and place it in the rack on their way out.

I grab myself a black Sharpie marker and get all the supplies I will need ready. I have to remember to label the urine tube I give the patient. I take a quick look around as I head to the front to get the requisition and call my first patient. I see a couple of phlebotomists that are apparently new. I hate seeing new people because I usually end up drawing the patient after they tried and missed. By this time the patient is angry and afraid, as well as hungry.

I see Bill drawing in the chair next to me. He is an experienced phlebotomist and a funny guy. I cannot say enough about how important a good sense of humor is in this line of work. I see a new young guy working in the front draw room. He says his name is Andy and his father is a doctor across the street at the hospital.

So over here at our main lab there are four people drawing blood plus people in the back who do the processing and run the tests. I think I could get spoiled over here. Liz and I agreed to call each other after work and compare notes. I call my first patient. Gracie Brown. I say good morning as I bring her back to my draw chair. She seems a little nervous and carries a tote bag, a heavy coat and an umbrella.

I am looking for a place to put her stuff, as I have a little tiny spot and people are walking past me from the back part of the office where the processing is done. I locate a spot. There is a room behind me and it is right next door to Sheryl's' office. The room holds supplies, has a sink and a window looking out to the parking lot plus a draw chair and a table. I had her put her things on the table and then we got started.

Apparently I failed to notice that the name on the front of my lab coat said David. My patient, Gracie, asks me if I am one of those people who used to be a man?

I was a little puzzled when she asked and then she pointed

out the name on my coat. I let her know that I have always been a woman. I explain that I am helping out and normally work at the office down in Whitney Park. "Oh" she says. "My veins roll honey and they always have a hard time getting the blood." "Okay" I say as I am feeling her veins. I find a perfectly good vein and draw her blood with no problem. As I am taping her arm she says "wow I barely felt anything." "Good, that's the way it is supposed to be" I tell her.

I go up to call my next patient. William Smith. "Hi Mr. Smith, how are you doing today?" "I am hanging in young lady" he says. "Are you new here?" he asks. "I have never seen you here before?" "I work at a different office and am filling in here this week" I let him know.

As I am looking at his order and getting the tubes ready I feel something wet on the right side of my face by my ear. I look over and Bill is standing at the drinking fountain flicking water at me. He seems to really be enjoying this and my patient has not noticed that the whole right side of my face is dripping with water. Looks like we will be having fun over here today. I draw my patient and give him instructions about collecting the urine in the cup and then pouring into a tube I have labeled with his name.

I just met a crazy funny black gal who is now working next to me in the hall. Her name is Towanda. She has dreadlocks today. I have never seen any body's hair braided like that before. She also has long claw like fingernails.

I call my next patient. "Good morning Mrs. Sweeney. How are you today?" "Well, I don't know" she says. "That is why I have to do lab work. I have no appetite and cannot seem to sleep all night anymore" she says. "Young lady do you think I am dying?" I tell her I have no idea. I bandage her arm and she heads up to the front to leave. As I follow her up to the front I notice a bit of a traffic jam ahead of us. Well this is unbelievable. If I was not seeing this myself I would have trouble believing it. My last patient, Mr. Smith is standing in the hall facing the rack of urine tubes. He is urinating straight into the tube while the tube is sitting in the rack. Patients are going around him with their walkers. Seriously? I say to myself.

It seems as if none of the patients have noticed what he is doing. I go into the first room and ask Bill if he can explain to this man that in the future he must go inside the bathroom. Bill is tied up so I must tell him.

When I approach Mr. Smith he is stuffing his penis back inside his pants and zipping up. There is a preservative inside each tube. It is a very tiny pill. Easy to miss it is so small. I am looking at his tube and I ask him if there was a tiny pill in the tube? "Yes" he says "I just swallowed it before I started." I said "you did what?" He says it again. He says "I thought it was a pill for me." I try and explain to him that it is a preservative to keep his urine fresh. He does not seem to understand or care. I have no idea what to do. I grab some gloves and carry his tube of urine and a few others in the rack to the back so it can get processed right away.

Wow this is going to be most interesting working here.

I walk into the first room and tell Bill what just happened. He says "no way, are you kidding?" Bill is fun to talk to and work with. He is old school like me and has twenty years experience. Bill and I are standing there talking and he says he needs to go do blood tests across the street tomorrow at the mental health locked unit. He asks if I want to help him? I said sure. This should be a new fun experience.

So Bill explains to me how it goes across the street. Apparently these patients are locked up for various reasons and he says this will be a fun gig that I will never forget.

I call my next patient. She has a glucose tolerance test for four hours. This is where we give her a very sweet soda like beverage to drink and we draw her blood every hour on the hour to see how her body reacts to all the sugar. We do these a lot for young women who are pregnant and may be getting gestational diabetes. I draw her blood first then I give her the drink. She must stay in the lab so we can watch her in case something happens. I explain the procedure to her and wait for her to finish the drink. I will draw her blood again in an hour. When I bring her back she does not look right. Before I can even get my stuff ready she is vomiting. I grab the garbage can. She says she is feeling like she might pass out. I ask Bill to help me get her into our room with an exam table to lay her down after she is done vomiting.

We also use that table to do EKG's. I forgot I would have to do those too while working at the main lab. I am starting to miss the Scrabble game at my regular office.

As we get her to the door and open the door there are two phlebotomists inside with a bunch of food from Taco Bell spread out on the table. When they see us they jump up and throw all the food in bags and change the paper on the table and practically run out of there. I crack open the window for some fresh air, thinking she probably is not going to want the Taco Bell smell.

Now I have to call the doctor and see if they want to cancel the test? I see Bill is checking on our patient, so I call the doctors office. Sara says cancel the test. I mark this on the requisition and then head to our room to inform our patient that she can go when she feels up to it. I help her up and she heads out.

Bill is taking orders for lunches and asks if I want to go with him to get Mexican food? Sure why not. We decide to eat ours there and then bring the others back their food. Then we will cover for them so they can eat in peace. Bill is a fun person. He is tall, dark and handsome and has the same amount of experience as I do. That is rare in this field. This is a nice break from my regular office. So we had a nice lunch and then we bring back everyone's orders.

We bring back about eight orders of Mexican food for people in the main lab. Bill and I tell them that we will hold down the fort while they all went outside to eat. So Bill and I sat up front where the secretaries sit and tried to figure out how to do the patients' paperwork and then we took turns drawing their blood.

It is pretty funny with us both trying to figure out how to get the patients registered. We normally only draw the blood. Guess we will not have both front office girls go to lunch at the same time again.

A young man comes in to do a semen analysis for fertilization. It involves him collecting his semen in a urine cup. They are checking to see if he has any live sperm or is shooting blanks.

I try to not make him any more uncomfortable than he already is so I do the paperwork and tell him to take a seat and let Bill call him back. I could hear parts of the conversation. I could hear him asking if we had any porn magazines for him to look at? Bill tells him no.

I hear the young man closing the door and Bill comes walking out. We talk for a few minutes and Bill motions for me to follow him into the first room. I had a puzzled look on my face and then Bill walks over and jiggles the handle on the bathroom door. I said "oh no" you are so mean! I am picturing this poor guy in the bathroom trying to collect his semen in the cup. Men can be just as mean as women. I really felt sorry for this poor man. Eventually the poor guy walks out and gives bill his sample.

This is quite interesting. I am restocking my draw station with tubes, needles and cotton and realize we are out of several different tubes. So while Bill was drawing somebody he directed me to supplies upstairs. I take the elevator upstairs to the second floor and I get to have a look at the two clowns who work in supplies. The two guys who sent me sixty thousand butterflies for one week down in Whitney Park. As I expected, they are two young guys. They look to be about twelve years old. I can hear them in the back laughing and boxes falling. I see a phone sitting on the counter. It's the perfect opportunity to catch Liz before she leaves the lab.

When she says hello, I say "hi stranger." She sounded awful. Apparently both Steffy and Dotty were late and she has drawn sixty people and each of them has drawn ten. First thing she said was "when the hell are you coming back down here?" I told her that hopefully next week. I told her to stop helping Dotty and Steffy and let them make mistakes so Sheryl will get lots of complaints. She agrees and we hang up. I agree to call in a day or two.

She tells me that they have had so many people today who were just not with it at all. Wow, I feel really bad that Liz is having to work with Dotty and Steffy. As I hang up the phone I see one of the two twelve year old supply guys bringing me several cartons of different colored tubes. I thank them and head back downstairs to the lab.

As I walk in through the side door into the back of the lab I notice that there are not too many tubes of blood in the rack in the processing area. That makes me very happy because it indicates a fairly slow day so far. I am afraid to say that out loud as it might suddenly get crazy busy. I see Towanda is drawing blood from somebody in the hallway and they are discussing hairdo's. Towanda is another phlebotomist with long red claw like nails. I see her frequently dropping tubes, tape and other things.

I head to the front room and announce that there are new tubes if anybody needs them. Apparently Bill has locked Andy in the supply closet. It is fun working with younger people over here. They love pranks. I see another phlebotomist that I don't really know is bringing a patient back to her draw chair, which is located next to the supply closet. Bill unlocks the door and Andy slips out the door as the patient is being seated in the chair.

Time for us to act like the professionals we appear to be in our white lab coats. As I restock my draw station I see Towanda is on a break and Andy is using her draw station.

As he sits down on his stool and gets ready to draw a patient I think I would try out a game Andy and I have played a few times before. So I bend over him and say "hey, don't forget to tie the tourniquet on and have you figured out which needle size you think you need?" He smiles and says "oh okay thanks for the help." At this point the twenty something girl asks him if he is new? She is looking a bit worried. So he gives the standard reply for this game.

"No, I did someone yesterday, you are my fifth person to draw." He is checking her veins and getting ready to draw this poor girl and I say "don't forget to uncap the needle." Now she looks even more nervous.

I chuckle as I go to see if there is a patient registered that I can call back. Andy is pretty fun to work with because he does not really need the job. His dad is a doctor and works at the hospital across the street. His father is trying to persuade him to go to medical school. Not seeing much interest yet. Andy works only a couple of afternoons a week, he likes to sleep in.

I call a young guy in his late twenties back. He takes a seat and I am getting things set up and ready to draw his blood when Bill walks by to the drinking fountain and says to me "oh hey your parole officer called while you were at lunch." The patient laughs. I think this is always nice to get someone who plays along and is pretty cool.

After I draw his blood I am labeling the tubes and I feel water hitting the side of my face. I glance over and here's Bill flicking water at my face from the drinking fountain once again. I am so close to the fountain I can reach it sitting down. I just smile and say "just you wait."

Meanwhile I tell Bill to go draw someone so the patient waiting behind him can get into the bathroom. The bathroom door is right next to the drinking fountain. This office is rather crowded.

I tape my patients arm and get ready to stand up and take my tubes to put them in the rack when I see Bill holding the door to the back office closed. Another fun lady who works in client services named Debbie is laughing on the other side of the door. I hear someone say Sheryl is here and boom all of a sudden Bill is back up front calling a patient back to draw their blood.

This is the same Sheryl who supervises us in Whitney

Park. Her office is directly across from my draw station. Sheryl is not here watching us all the time, but when she is here she is watching and listening to just about everything. I am reminded of why I like having my own office. Luckily I only have one more hour until I am off work. I walk down the hall and as I pass Sheryl's office I hear her say "hey Betty come in here please." I walk in and she says "hi Betty, I just got a phone call from Liz at Whitney park. She desperately needs you back down there. Betty I have a favor to ask."

"I need you to go to the Hemlock office and fill in for two weeks and then back to Whitney park. She says "I need you to see if you can see what the hell is going on out there? It is a very busy office and they do about one hundred and fifty geriatric patients per day, so I need to send someone who has the geriatric experience." She adds that we will pay your mileage, I know it is a bit of a drive. There are three phlebotomists and a supervisor who may be doing questionable things. I ask when she when she wants me to do this? "Day after tomorrow" she says. I know Bill could use your help across the street tomorrow. "Oh okay" I say.

Oh look at the time I am ready to head home.

CHAPTER

12

THE ALARM GOES OFF AT SIX A.M. and I am sure it is a dream. I wake up thirty minutes later to realize it was not a dream and I really need to scramble now to get to the main lab by seven. I hate to have to rush. I guess I will have to drive through someplace and eat while I drive. I seriously need some coffee if I am going to get through two hours in the mental health unit.

So now I have been sitting in traffic and it is still stop and go. Last time it was stop, I had to do a panic stop and now I have both an egg stain and a coffee stain on the front of my clean scrubs.

Love to start the day with huge stains on the front of my scrubs. This means all day long there will be questions from the patients' about what happened? As I roll into the parking lot for the main lab I notice all the spaces are full. I am going to be glad to not have to deal with this parking nightmare after today. I guess employees parking is not a priority. So I drive down the street looking for spots on the street. I end up parking on a side street by a pharmacy. Now I am ten minutes late.

As I walk into the back door of the lab it appears to be very busy. Phones are ringing and there are tubes of blood in racks waiting to be spun, this is not looking good. I grab a lab coat and head down the hall towards the front. I see Bill is using my draw station, so I stop at the drinking fountain and turn the water on and flick water with my thumb and forefinger into Bills ear. It took three times before he noticed. I thought this was a brilliant way to announce my arrival.

Bill says "we are slammed with patients, but around ten we will head across the street to the mental health unit. "Okay" I say. I set my stuff in the combination EKG, Taco Bell and everything else room and grab a requisition and call my first patient. There are only six chairs in the waiting room, so patients are hanging out outside the door. There looks to be about twelve patients waiting, but with four phlebotomists drawing it goes fast. I call Mr. Roy Barnes back just as Bill is done. He says "it is all yours" as he got up from my draw chair.

"Good morning Mr. Barnes" I say as he takes a seat in the draw chair. I take a look at his requisition as I put my gloves on. I see Mr. Barnes is very nervous, sweating profusely and still in his pajamas and slippers. His requisition is a standing order, which means he comes in regularly. I am starting to wonder if he walked out of a facility and will need help finding his way back. I tell him I will be right back. I go to the front room and locate Bill and ask him if he knows this patient? He says he will come and double check in a couple minutes.

Bill walks over and says "hi Roy, how are you doing, do

you recognize me?" No response. Bill informs me that Mr. Barnes belongs across the street at the mental health unit. So Bill says we can walk him back over when we go and that we should wait to draw his blood because he is here alone and they may not want it done today.

I see Bill grabbing a plastic box that looks like a tackle box. He is filling it up with tubes and needles and other supplies. He tells me to go grab one. So I get one and start filling it up with supplies. I ask Bill to keep an eye on Mr. Barnes while I use the bathroom. Now we are ready to walk across the street to the mental health unit. As we walk, Bill fills me in about how this will go. Apparently it is a locked unit and we are not allowed to be alone with a patient. There are two staff members that will be in the room and a third staff member will bring two patients in at a time. These patients can be unpredictable and can become violent. Holy cow, this is way above my pay grade. I will not be doing this again. Another experience that I will never forget.

As we approach the door, Bill rings the bell and a voice comes through the speaker. Bill announces that we are here to draw blood and that we have one of their patients with us. We hear a chuckle. A rather large woman opens the door for us to come in. Her name tag says Marcie. Marcie is wearing a top with what looks like monkeys all over it and she has on some black spandex bottoms. All appear to be about three sizes too small. Her hair is several shades of blonde and is up in a bun. "Roy how did you get over there?" she asks. "Thanks for bringing him back."

As we walk in there is a dry erase board that says "today is Tuesday and it is sunny outside," with a picture drawn of a yellow sun. This gives me a slight clue as to what we are in for.

Marcie motions for us to follow her to the room we will use to draw the blood. As we walk down the hall we can see patients doing a variety of things. Some are watching TV while others are peacefully staring at the wall or ceiling. At the end of the hall we see an older man and woman sneak into what appears to be a closet. There are two men at a table discussing loudly which one has the higher hand in a card game. OOPS one of them just punched the other in the face, knocking him to the ground. One thing is for sure, I will most likely remember this day for quite some time.

Marcie says oh that's Dennis and Marvin. They fight all day over cards. She didn't seem alarmed that one of them was lying on the floor. "Okay here is your room" she says. She places a walkie talkie on the counter and says if you need anything or need to use the bathroom let me know. Someone has to escort you and unlock the door. Okay I will send two people in to supervise and watch the patients to make sure they do not have an outburst. We do not want either of you to get hurt. I just look at Bill like what the hell? He just smiles.

So Bill and I decide where we want to set up our stuff. There is a four foot long table, so we agree to each put a chair at each end of the table. We can stand side by side in the middle while drawing our patients. In walks the two workers. One is a chubby thirtyish man with short brown hair and a cigarette tucked on top of his right ear. The other is a somewhat overweight young woman in her twenties with tattoos and long blonde hair. She looks pretty tough. I do not want to make her mad. They both just kind of nod to us. I guess they are not into conversation.

Now Marcie brings us the first two patients. The male is wearing bathing trunks, fins for swimming and a motorcycle helmet. She seats him in Bill's chair. Bill is not making conversation. Next she brings me a young female who is wearing flannel pajamas and flip flops. She is rocking back and forth and looking at the ceiling. They are all having a drug level test and all we need is one lavender tube for each patient.

Bill is almost finished with his first patient while I am getting ready to draw my patients blood. I steady her arm and just go for it. I use a butterfly needle because they move with the patient a little. We often use them on babies and children because there is tubing attached to the needle and you can actually let go of the needle once you are in the vein. This is helpful since these patients are a bit unpredictable.

Okay, all done with this patient. As she shuffles out, Marcie is at the door with two more patients. We each are given a young man approximately twenty years old. They seem to be a bit sedated so we are done quickly. Next I get a young girl who appears very agitated. She is hopping on one foot as she comes in the door. Marcie comes and speaks to her quietly and reminded her that she needs to sit still for a couple minutes.

She is able to sit still for about one minute until she starts asking me questions, one after another. What's my name? What am I here for? The questions keep coming.

I have everything ready and I ask her to please hold still. As I start tying the tourniquet around her arm she starts screaming at me, saying "oh my God you touched my breast. Are you a lesbian?" I am standing there speechless when the two workers walk over, stand next to the young lady calmly asking her if she could stay still so the nice lady can finish drawing her blood.

I look over at Bill and he is smiling. Actually when you are tying a tourniquet on a woman you can sometimes brush the side of her breast.

I ask the young lady if she would rather have Bill draw her blood instead of me? She said she needs to think about it. Wow this is a new one for me. So literally for five minutes she sat there looking at Bill and then at me. She finally decided that she would allow me to draw her blood. So she moved her arm as far out from her body as she could and I was able to finish drawing her blood and she was on her way.

We only have four more patients to draw and we are done.

Next Marcie brings us two men. Mine seems to be in his forties and he is dressed in a brown military camouflage uniform. He is mumbling under his breath something about being under attack. I manage to get the blood drawn quickly. As he heads out the door he is crouching down along the wall.

I flag down Marcie and ask to be escorted to the bathroom. I think I will let Bill finish up. As I exit the bathroom Bill is just finishing up with the last patient.

We head back across the street with the blood. Well, this has given me a whole new appreciation for the patients I usually deal with. The good news is it is lunch time. I am going to walk around the corner to the taco place. I am very hungry. Boy what a strange morning this was. I am thinking how much it would suck if I had to be closed up in that mental health unit with those people for eight hours a day.

I order myself a huge burrito and a coke. I deserve it. At this restaurant you place your order, pay and take a seat. They give you chips and a number when you pay and you can get salsa yourself at a self serve bar while you wait for them to bring you your order. Boy it sure feels good to get away from the office for lunch.

Unfortunately I am fifteen minutes late returning from

lunch, but I really feel justified since I had no morning break.

As I head down the hallway to put my stuff away I see Bill and Andy are in the front room and Towanda is at the draw station next to me in the hallway. I am wearing a lab coat that belongs to someone named Cheryl. There is another girl drawing in the EKG room.

I head to the closet to get some urine specimen cups. The closet is located next to the second draw chair in the front room and I have to slide in sideways to get into the closet to the get the cups since Andy is drawing somebody at that chair. There is no light in the closet for some reason. I keep one foot trying to hold the door open and as I reach further back into the closet the door slams shut. Damn, it has to be Bill who did this. I push hard but it is not budging. Bill must be holding it shut. I guess Bill and Andy have both finished drawing their patients and are having some fun. They could not be drawing a patient and holding the door shut at the same time.

I yell out "Bill damn you, open this door right now." I hear Andy Laughing. At least this lab is not boring, right? So Bill says "what's the secret password?" I am thinking what the hell? We are adults here aren't we? I hear a woman's voice. She is asking Bill if he is alright? I guess he must look strange holding the door shut. She is one of the secretaries from the front and she starts laughing when she realizes what is going on. All of a sudden I hear Sheryl's voice saying "Bill what the hell are you doing?"

Oh thank God! Saved by Sheryl. Now I feel the door release and Sheryl calling Bill out to the hallway. She says she has a job for him. I am laughing my ass off. I think Sheryl knows what he was doing. Somehow I get the feeling he does this to other people regularly.

I see the bathroom light on under the bathroom door. Andy must have slipped into the bathroom fast when he heard Sheryl's voice. I have to say the fun part of working here is that I am not the lead Phlebotomist. I just draw patients and have fun with Andy and Bill. I will miss these two characters. We tend to act like teenagers and Sheryl has to babysit us in between actually drawing blood and taking care of patients.

I start stocking my draw station with supplies. When there are no patients you have to look busy, otherwise Sheryl finds some dumb job for you to do. I head to the bathroom by my draw station and I see Bill in the back spinning tubes of blood in the centrifuge. I give him a thumbs up as I walk into the bathroom and he laughs.

As I am washing my hands I hear someone knocking at the door, someone who probably has to collect a specimen. Geez, we need private employee bathrooms. When possible I head up to the third floor where there is a one seater bathroom in the hallway. When Sheryl is not here it is easy.

As I head towards the front I see Sheryl gathering her stuff in her office. Woo hoo she must be leaving.

I see a requisition on the counter and get ready to draw my next patient. No sooner do I get the patient into the draw chair when Andy walks over and takes a seat in the first chair. You know what this means? Time for some fun with my young female patient. Her name is Lisa and she is in her early twenties. Andy's favorite type for this game. As I am checking her veins and making light easy conversation with her Andy says "do you need help tying the tourniquet?" I say "I think I got it." Well Lisa picked right up on it and is looking a bit nervous. She asks me if I am new? I say yes.

She said how new? I say "I did three people yesterday."

She starts to sweat. Andy leans over and tells her that it will be alright, then he says to me "hey don't forget to clean her arm, and uncap the needle." This poor girl is looking so upset I finally tell her that we are teasing her, and that I have twenty years experience. I thank her for being such a great sport in our little game. She laughs. So I finish drawing her blood and tell her to have a nice rest of her day. I motion through the glass window asking Bill to come over here. I let him know that Sheryl is gone. He smiles.

Fifteen minutes later Bill walks through the door. It's going to be a fun two hours until it is time to go. Andy is drawing a patient, but there is nobody waiting. It is usually quiet from two to four p.m., then it gets real busy from four to six p.m. with after work people. Believe it or not every so often we get a patient that comes in after work for a fasting test.

Time for me to saunter into the front room and see if Andy needs any help?

Oh this looks like it might be fun. Andy has just picked the spot where he plans to draw his patient's blood. This lady looks to be about forty years old. So I walk up behind Andy and stand over by the closet and I say, "how are you doing here? Do you remember the bounce and feel of the vein?" he says "Ya, I think so." A vein actually feels like pushing on an inflated balloon. His patient is looking a bit unsure at this point. I say "okay, don't forget to take the tourniquet off before you take the needle out."

If you don't get the tourniquet off at the right time the blood starts coming out too fast. This is a lot of fun. Now his patient is asking him if he has done this before? He is trying to assure her he has done this many times and we are just joking around. I walk over and tell her it is true. We were just having a little fun with her.

My goodness we need to lay off this game for awhile, before it gets back to Sheryl. Sheryl already treats us like we are her kids and that she has to keep us in line. Which is not far from the truth. Actually Sheryl is only about four or five years older than I am. It is hard to explain but this job can be so serious that we have to try and make things fun, or the day just drags on and on.

Okay, this patient appears to be doing a little better with our silly game. I thank her for being a good sport. I let her know that I have twenty years of experience and that I could draw her if it would make her feel more comfortable?

She is liking this idea so I go ahead and draw her blood. Andy is good with the idea because then hopefully neither one of us will get chewed out by Sheryl. I give the lady a real nice draw. I use the butterfly needle so she will not feel anything and will barely even have a mark on her arm. This way she will leave with a good feeling. Geez Louise!

I am starting to think about tomorrow. I have no idea what I am in for over at this other outpatient office in Hemlock, California. I didn't even know we had an office there. It is a boring little town and ninety percent of the residents are senior citizens. I will have a long one hour drive, at least they are paying my mileage. I sure do miss my real office.

Things are pretty slow right now so I head for the EKG room to sit and call Liz. I have to find out what's going on in Whitney Park? Liz is already gone for the day so I call her at home. She says she is ready to quit. Apparently they have Liz opening the lab so she has to come in half an hour earlier. She is not happy about that because there is more traffic at eight a.m. than there is at her usual 8:30 a.m.

I tell Liz that I have to drive all the way to the Hemlock office starting tomorrow. Liz says "Oh my God, I have heard that it is a crazy busy office and the phlebotomists are real strange out there." "Well one thing for sure, I will have lots of stories to tell you when I get back" I say.

She says "well I have plenty stories for you. Steffy is now wearing black hair and black nails and the really old patients think something is wrong with her. One old man asked me if she had like a disease or something? Yesterday I had to send her home to change shoes. She had on black high heels and she got the heel tangled up in a thread that was hanging out of the carpet in the waiting room. She was stuck in place for a few minutes in front of four patients."

I decide to be funny and ask Liz if she has a broomstick parked in the corner? I get a brief laugh out of her. Liz asks me if the patients are always piled up against the front door in the morning. "Yep" I say. I tell her that I should be back in two weeks. Liz says she will call in sick for the next few days.

I ask Liz if she personally knows any of the phlebotomists at the Hemlock office? She says no. She has just heard rumors. "Oh by the way, Cedrick was peeing on the front of the building earlier today in his usual fashion and an old lady was walking by and called the police. I think he got a citation" says Liz. "Oh wow, he has been doing that for at least five years."

"Oh, and I forgot to tell you yesterday that I went out the back door of Urgent Care for some fresh air and saw Bill and Jackie having sex out back behind the loading dock. "Did they see you?" "No, but it was a close call" Liz says.

Liz continues "And I am sick of working all day. No wonder you are bitchy at the end of the day." Liz has to work full days when I am gone because she, Bill and I are the only phlebotomists that know how to draw babies and the tough elderly patients with very small veins.

" I almost forgot to tell you," says Liz "two days ago I walked to the door to open up at eight a.m. and there was another phlebotomist there from another office. So I called the main lab and Steve, the guy who does scheduling, said he thought I was on vacation this week? Can you believe it?" "Yes, after working here for six years I can honestly say that nothing surprises me" I tell Liz.

We talk for a few more minutes and Liz tells me that she heard that the supervisor or lead person out in Hemlock frequently has visits from her husband as well as her boyfriend during working hours and the other phlebotomists cover for her. "Well this will be most interesting" I say to Liz. We say goodbye and agree to catch up next week on all the sordid details. We also agree that once I get back and we get settled back into our routine it will be time for us to plan another beach day together.

As I walk out of the EKG room I notice it is almost four p.m. I gather my things and head to the bathroom on my way out. "Holy cow, whoever used this bathroom last has made a mess. There is urine on the floor at the base of the toilet, urine on the sink and one of those white plastic hats that sits on the outside of the toilet rim to catch the urine or feces has been left on the floor. I try to find someone to notify about this mess before I leave. Someone has to clean it up because the cleaning crew only comes at night. Thank goodness it is time for me to go home. We are open until six p.m. and I think Bill is closing up this week. Okay I am done for the day. Bill and Andy are trying to bribe Towanda to clean the bathroom as I walk out the door.

CHAPTER

1 3

TODAY MY ALARM GOES OFF AT FIVE THIRTY a.m. This must be a mistake? I lay there in shock. Oh that's right I have to go to Hemlock. This is way above my pay grade here. When I get finished here Sheryl had better give me that raise or I will not do this again.

I guess once again I will have to drive through McDonald's because it is a one hour drive and the office opens at seven a.m. and apparently the line goes out the door and around the corner. Apparently all the patients are geriatric patients. They use lots of butterfly needles because old people's veins are small generally speaking and the patients are frequently dehydrated which makes it difficult to find a vein. I drag myself out to the car with several water bottles and snack bars and twenty bucks. Man I hope these people are easy to work with.

Okay I am almost there. I was given specific directions on how to find the Hemlock lab and where to park by some guy named Doug who works there as a phlebotomist. I was told to come in off Elm, a side street, and look for a back door marked with the letter B and park next to a white Mitsubishi SUV. He also described two other cars for me to look for. Okay I see the cars and the B on the back door. I guess this is it. Apparently all of the employees enter through the back door and there is another parking lot off another street that the patient's park in.

The whole back area here is all gravel. As I climb out and head to the door I notice the white SUV says "Bridled but never tamed" around the license plate, interesting! I wonder who drives that car? There's another red four door compact car that has a gray front end on the passenger side and four tires that are all different brands. There is another gray car with the rear end smashed in. Yes, I will definitely fit in parking my nineteen ninety nine Subaru forester back here.

I knock at the back door but there is no answer. I try the handle and it is open. I walk into a dark wood paneled room with a desk and a couple of chairs. There are several phlebotomists and we all introduce ourselves. I explain that Sheryl sent me here to help out. They all laugh. Not sure about that?

So far everyone seems pretty nice. They are drinking coffee and eating donuts. They all say help yourself. We have ten more minutes before we have to open the front door.

There is Amber, she is petite with red hair and seems to be very friendly and helpful. Another woman named Rena. She is a nice looking, stocky black gal. Sally who is apparently the supervisor is very tall with fake blonde hair in a short sassy looking style, tight black pants and black boots.

Next a young guy of about thirty walks through the door already in a lab coat, who appears to be ushering a very elderly man out the back door. He says hello, his name is Doug. He is a rather overweight guy with a receding hairline. As the elderly man walks out I learn that he is a patient and Doug has worked out some kind of a deal with him where he brings a dozen donuts to the back door and he gets his blood drawn without waiting in the super long line in the front.

This looks like a fun bunch to me. They have found me a lab coat in one of the closets. It is seven a.m. and we are all walking up front, apparently it is the same as Whitney Park, each and every patient is in a desperate hurry to have their blood drawn so they may eat. Okay so Sally is registering patients at the front desk and I can see the line is going out the door. There are about fifteen chairs for patients to sit in.

We have about ten more minutes before Sally gets a few patients registered. Amber gives me a tour and it is a real old looking office with lots of paneling in the waiting room and only one bathroom. There are two blood draw rooms, one in the front and one in the back. Each has two chairs and the bathroom is in the hall. I think I better use the bathroom before we start.

Amber shows me the processing room which is the size of a small walk-in closet and where I can put my stuff. I am told that Amber and Rena take turns processing and Doug does whatever. Sally sits up front and registers people and not much actual drawing of the blood. Amber says I can draw in the large room in the back with Doug.

I see which chair Doug is using and I take the other chair. Doug is talking with his male patient about fishing. So this is interesting, forty elderly people waiting and Doug is casually talking about fishing. I call my first patient back, Mabel Smith. "Good morning Mrs. Smith" I say as we walk down the hall. Mabel is ninety two years old. She is here for several tests, one of which is her lipid panel. I cannot imagine being ninety two years old and being concerned about my cholesterol, just saying. I help her put her things down on the exam table and help her into the draw chair. I get my needle and alcohol and tubes ready and put the tourniquet on her tiny bony arm and start looking for a vein I can use. Doug has a round stool to sit on and so do I. This is quite relaxing.

"So Mabel, do you have someone waiting for you?" "Yes honey, my son is out in the car." "Okay good" I say. Mabel asks "are you new?" I tell her that I am new to this office but that I have twenty years experience drawing blood. I let her know that I was asked to come help out because it is such a busy office. She seems content with that explanation. I finish up and tape her arm and help her get her things together and place them on top of the seat on her walker. I ask her if she thinks she can get me a urine specimen before she goes? I label her cup and help her to the bathroom and give her instructions. I walk to the front to ask Sally where they have the patients leave their urine specimens? "Well we don't really have a spot so you just have to watch for your patient to come out and take it to the processing room before you go on to the next patient." "Okay, thanks" I say.

Wow, this is hard to believe that there is no rack and only one bathroom. I see there is still a line of four people. No wonder the line is so long in the lobby. So after she comes out of the bathroom I take her urine to processing and then I help her out to the lobby.

As I go to the front counter to get the paperwork for another patient I notice that Sally is on a personal call with her feet up on the desk drinking coffee and eating a donut, all while the other phone line is ringing. No way am I going to stop drawing a patient in order to answer the other phone line.

I see Rena and Amber are having fun in the front room.

They are entertaining two female patients. Each one of them has a patient in their draw chair. These two seem to have a little game going. Rena is pretending to be kind of crazy in the head and then Amber swoops in with a syringe, containing only water, pretends to give Rena a shot and then Rena goes back to acting normal. The two female patients are thoroughly enjoying this. It actually might be fun working here. They see me watching and I give them a thumbs up.

My next patient is an eighty three year old lady dressed in a red hat and red outfit. I guess she is part of that red hat society. Very cute. Her name is Marjorie Phelps. So I help her put her stuff on the bed and let her take a seat. I see a patient in Doug's chair but no sign of Doug. As I am getting ready to draw Ms. Phelps blood Doug comes walking up to his patient with his fishing pole in his hand and some lures in his other hand. My patient is smiling and says her husband is a fisherman too.

Apparently this lab is in a league of its own. You know these patients seem more normal than the ones we get in Whitney Park. Just saying. Maybe there really is something in the drinking water at Whitney Park?

After drawing her blood I tape my patient's arm and show her to the door. As the door closes Amber and Rena come up to the counter where I am standing and say "watch this." Amber gets a blank requisition and marks some tests and as she is giggling she says "what do ya think?" Rena and I both laugh.

They have just created a fake patient for Doug. So for first name they put URA and last name Dick. Then they stick a sticky note on it with Doug's name on it making it look like someone requested him. Amber sticks it on top of the pile so we can all have a laugh. A couple of minutes later here comes Doug up to the front to call his next patient. I have to say this is hilarious. Took him three times of calling a patient by the name of URA Dick before he realizes it is a joke.

Everyone is enjoying this. Sally is still talking on the phone. The patients are looking a bit restless and agitated because they are hungry. So apparently this is the norm here, where Sally doesn't do much and everyone else picks up the slack.

I head down the hall with another patient. I see the back door open and Sally heading out to her car. Okay, so the white SUV with "Bridled but never tamed" around the license plate is hers."

I now have a seemingly nice patient named Marvin Jones. He is about sixty five and has dreadlocks and a set of ear buds in. Boy the age of these patients varies greatly. So Marvin and I make light conversation while I get ready to draw his blood. Marvin is a musician who plays drums in a band on Saturday nights in another town nearby. Very amusing. He says all the baby boomers come in to listen to them play. I finish drawing Marvin's blood and as we walk out to the hall he says "oh hey is that a back door? Can I just slip out the back, then I won't have to walk all the way around?" "Sure no problem" I say as I walk him to the door.

Well as I open the door for him to go out we see Sally in her SUV in the front seat with her back to us. Geez Louise a closer look reveals a man underneath her and she is moving up and down. Marvin is smiling and I am looking like a deer in the headlights. Honestly, this is another situation that has not come up before at work. I wonder who the guy is? He has long blonde hair and that is all I can see. I wonder if it her husband? Marvin is still watching them and looks like he would like to get in on the fun. I wish him well and head back inside.

I cannot believe this woman, Sally.

Looks like the patients are cleared out of the waiting room. Doug is taking orders for a food run across the street to a hamburger stand. I order a cheeseburger and a coke and offer to kick in towards onion rings and zucchini sticks and ranch sauce. Sounds delish.

So after Doug heads out I pull Amber aside and ask a few questions about Sally. Apparently this is a frequent occurrence. I describe what I saw. Amber says oh really? Again? Amber says matter of factly "blonde hair is the boyfriend, brown hair is the husband." Amber asks if I can sit at the desk while she finishes processing the blood. I say "sure." Apparently Rena is on a break and is out walking. Boy this is turning out to be an interesting place for sure. So apparently there are no designated breaks in this office, it is a free for all. Amber said we take turns going into the back room to munch and then if you need to run an errand you just let them know. Sounds like most of the work and patient load is from seven to eleven a.m. Just a few here and there in the afternoon.

Good thing I am only here for a week or two because I would soon not be able to fit into my scrubs eating like this. So I am checking out the front desk area. The whole waiting room looks like it is from the fifties. Wood paneling everywhere and old funky chairs. Seems like the place has been all but forgotten.

I see a closet off of the front office, it has a door that slides shut. I open the door and peek in. Well looky here, Sally has got a whole closet with personal stuff. Makeup, clothes, candy etc. Her purse is in here too. She must have been in a real hurry to get out back. This is getting real interesting.

Doug is back with lunch, so I am scooting to the back room as Sally passes me going down the hall. She looks like she has just run a marathon, quite flushed and hair all messed up. This woman has no shame.

This is hilarious.

Sally can cover the front desk for awhile. Wow this food is really good. Not sure what I will say to Sheryl about this situation. We all are pigging out on the food when Sally walks in the back room. Did you save me anything? Doug gives her a zucchini stick. She says I didn't know you ordered food? Doug pipes up with "I hated to knock on your car window and disturb you." She gave a nervous laugh. She quickly announces that she is going to go get a sandwich and will be right back.

After she leaves everybody starts talking amongst themselves saying I wonder if her husband knows?

Amber heads up front to watch for patients. She eats like a parakeet, no wonder she has such a cute figure, and the three of us still munching away do not. The door opens to the back room and it is Amber. She says Sally's husband is here looking for her? Oh my, the plot thickens. He is sitting in the lobby waiting for her to return. I take my coke and head up to the front. Doug says he has to run to his house and will be right back.

Amber is getting ready to leave for the day. About fifteen minutes later Sally comes walking in the back door with a drink in her hand. As she gets to the front I let her know that her husband is here to see her. She looks at me with a strange oops kind of look. She brings her husband into the back room. This is freaking unbelievable. Rena is registering a patient that I guess I will draw since there is nobody else available. I call our lone patient back. Mr. Jack Wagner.

"Good afternoon Mr. Wagner how are you?" I say. "Well young lady not too bad" he says. He asks "Where's the big guy?" Oh he went out to run an errand. "He and I are planning on going fishing pretty soon." "Oh nice." I say. So Mr. Wagner is just in for a protime to make sure his blood is not too thin. After I finish up and get his arm taped he says "I think I will hang out for a few and talk to Doug when he comes in." "Okay" I say and I see him head out the back door.

I guess Sandy and her husband are finishing with lunch. I hear Mr. Wagner say hello as he walks through. The door is now opened to the back room. I head up to the front counter to see if there are any patients? Nice and quiet. I find out Rena is a wife and mother who also sings in a band of some sort. All of a sudden we hear commotion. I hear children. Rena says she is really tired and would I mind checking the back?

"Sure, no problem," I say. As I head down the hall several two to three year olds come running towards me. I say hello to them and they run back out the back door. I see Doug is back with his boat. Doug has triplets. Just the thought of that makes me tired. Apparently he is using the garden hose on the outside of the building to wash his boat out. Mr. Wagner is helping and visiting. Doug has on a pair of Khakis pants and a Hawaiian shirt. Rena says he will come in and draw if we need him. All we have to do is call him. Wow, I thought we were relaxed in Whitney Park. This is wild.

As I walk up front I see Sally is now sitting at the desk and

Rena is sitting in the extra chair. I stand at the front counter and make small talk. Sally has her head inside her little closet/room and is eating some bagged popcorn. Here come Doug's kids again. They are running up and down the hallway and it literally sounds like a daycare center in here. Sally is looking annoyed, but not saying anything. A patient walks in and Rena gets up and heads to the back.

All of a sudden it is quiet. Doug has lifted the kids up and put them in the boat. Apparently Doug's girlfriend is at a doctors appointment and there was nobody to watch the kids.

Sally is talking with this male patient at the window. Apparently he has a test called an AFP test. Sally is telling him that his doctor must have made a mistake because this test is for female patients who are pregnant. She tries to call the doctors office which is two doors down but the line is busy.

So Sally advises this man to double check on the test at the doctors office. He heads out the door and Sally goes back to her bag of popcorn. Sally offers Rena and I some popcorn. We are just chatting when this same male patient walks back in the door. We all say hello again. He hands Sally the requisition again. Same thing. She asks him what the doctors office said? Well the doctor was busy with a patient and the office girls said for me to tell you this is the right test.

Sally tries the phone number again and it is still busy. Sally and Rena shrug their shoulders and ask the patient to go back and double check with the doctor, not the office girls. Holy cow, this is bordering on ridiculous. I hate to make them look stupid in front of the patient and risk alienating them and making them angry, but I may have no choice. I cannot believe these women do not know this and do not have the sense to look it up.

Fifteen minutes later the man walks in the door again with the requisition and he is very angry. I say "ugh Sally, I think I may know what the problem is here." She looks at me like I have three heads. I say "Sally, I know the AFP test can be for men also. In men the test is a tumor marker." Bingo!

Sally looks a bit annoyed and irritated. I think this is the most work I have seen her do. So Sally is looking it up on the computer to see what color tube to use and how much blood we need and if it needs to be frozen or kept at room temperature to send to the main lab with the courier. The man is now seated in the lobby looking very agitated. I decide to go to the bathroom and let Rena draw his blood. I will offer to process the blood for her. I will have to mention to Sheryl something about Sally being very lazy and ignorant and not sure about the husband/boyfriend situation.

I come out of the bathroom and can hear Rena in the front draw room trying to smooth things over with this poor man. This will undoubtedly result in a complaint to Sheryl. Sally is suddenly not talking to me at all. This is what happens when you know something the lead person does not know. Egos are a huge problem in the medical field. Sally does not seem to be much of a team player.

Well looky here, it is three thirty and here comes Doug. Sally tells me I can go ahead and take off early if I want because Doug has not done anything all day and I have been doing his share. Well I have an hour drive ahead so I say thank you and am on my way.

We will see what tomorrow brings? I am thinking I better have soup for dinner because of all the calories I ingested at lunch.

CHAPTER

WHEN I GET HOME I CALL LIZ and tell her all about my day. She cannot hardly believe what I am telling her. She is intrigued by the Sally story and is speechless when I tell her about Sally in her car out back. Liz is asking if we could take turns going to the Hemlock office because it sounds like more fun than our office.

Liz tells me that Mrs. Nelson was in today and tried telling her where to stick her with the needle. Now this is the woman who not only told me where to stick the needle but also told me that I had only one chance to get her blood. Well Liz did the same thing I did and sent her down to the main lab. Mrs. Nelson says she will not be back to our office. We will have to celebrate when I get back!

This happens with about every fiftieth patient. They walk in and tell you that you only get one chance to get their blood and then proceed to tell you which vein they want you to use. They almost always leave you frustrated and swearing under your breath. I cannot believe Liz reacted the same way. It is not easy to have a patient tell you how to do your job.

Liz says Cedrick is still peeing on the front of the building and that Mr. Wilson was in asking about me? She told him I will be back soon. Liz also tells me that a woman walking her dog came upon Jackie and Bill in a compromising position again out back by the loading dock. Apparently she made a complaint. Liz and I agree that we shall talk again soon and compare notes.

I am hearing a buzzing. I ignore it. Crap there it is again. It feels like I just went to bed and I can't believe it is five thirty a.m. already. I am glad these new hours are temporary. I head out thirty minutes later even though I feel like I have been run over by a train. I think I will go for a walk today to get out of the nut house for a bit.

As I roll into the parking area in the back of the lab I see a different little old man sitting on the seat of his walker holding a box of donuts. Oh geez this is shameful. What was Doug thinking? Thankfully Doug pulls up and opens the door and greets the man. I decide that I am going to hang in the car for five minutes while I go over in my mind what all took place yesterday in this crazy office.

I was just thinking about what happened when I arrived home at my apartment yesterday. I live upstairs in an apartment with my eighteen year old son Jared. As I was walking up the stairs my neighbor, who lives downstairs, stopped me and mentioned something about the beautiful young girl living with me. As far as I know it is only my son and I sharing this two bedroom apartment. I do know that my sons girlfriend has been driving him home at night after he gets off at work at ten p.m. This has helped me out a lot because if she didn't I would have to go get him. We live thirty minutes outside of the city in the forest.

So apparently what has been happening is that after the girlfriend drives him home they both go into his bedroom for the night. At this point I am already asleep in my room and have no idea this is going on. Then I get up and leave for work around six a.m. before Jared is awake. I guess they get up after I leave and she drives him to school. Life has gotten interesting since he is eighteen and is now writing his own notes for absences at school. I guess they are hanging out in my apartment part of the day.

Now this is all making more sense in my mind. My apartment is all electric and my electric bill has been getting higher in the past few months and I couldn't figure out why? Geez Louise why didn't I see this sooner? Well no time to ponder this dilemma right now, as it is seven a.m. and I must go inside to work to pay for the electricity so my sons girlfriend can wash her beautiful long blonde hair and blow it dry forever!

The other issue I faced when I got home yesterday was a message on the answering machine from my mother saying she was sending a check for my son to use to go pick up his dog at the shelter. Apparently the dog got picked up again for roaming the neighborhood.

We have a beautiful English Springer named Freddie Freeloader and since the divorce and the move from a house with a fenced in yard Freddie has had to get used to an apartment with a doggie door. I don't have the money to bail Freddie Freeloader out every time because I am spending all my money on the electric bill.

Well my life is never boring, I will say that. As usual my mother also reminds me that I would make a lot more money as a nurse. She neglects to mention how I could pay for the schooling to make that happen.

As I walk in the back door to the lab there is coffee and donuts, a welcome treat. I help myself as I get my lab coat on and put my stuff away. Sally is doing the only real thing she does. Registering patients, oh I think she also orders supplies. Amber is puttering around in the processing room. Rena is running late as she had a singing engagement late last night. Hopefully Doug will do some more drawing blood today than he did yesterday.

There are two requisitions ready on the counter. Doug grabs one, I grab the other and I follow him back to our drawing room. Both of our patients are already seated in the draw chairs. Doug looks over at me to see how many tubes I am drawing on this man? As I glance over I see that we both are drawing two tubes on each of our patients. Doug turns to me and gives me a look that says go, so we both proceed to quickly draw our patients' blood. Holy cow, we are now racing each other without our patients realizing it. Wow! I have never done anything like this before. It appears like he has finished three seconds before me but his patient's arm is still bleeding, which means he has to hold pressure a bit longer until the bleeding stops before he can tape his patients' arm, so I win!

Well that was kind of fun. I have to say this place is not boring at all. We both head out towards the front following our patients and drop the blood tubes in the rack in the processing room.

I walk up to the front counter to see what is going on today? Amber and Rena are both drawing blood. Sally is continuing to register patients. The line is out the door. People are complaining loudly about the wait to whoever is listening.

Doug is still in the back, completely oblivious to the length of the line.

I head for the bathroom before calling another patient. I feel lucky that no one was in the bathroom. When I come out of the bathroom there are three people in line. As I head up to the front counter I hear some commotion. Someone in the lobby has collapsed on the floor and the paramedics have just arrived. Apparently two old ladies were fighting over their spot in the line. The other patients have stepped right over her and are up at the front counter. One has the sign-in clipboard and is crossing off the name of the patient who is on the ground and putting her own name in that spot. Another lady is trying to grab the clipboard away from her.

Two old men have set up a card game in the corner. People are seated on the seats of their walkers because all the chairs are occupied. Sally has stopped registering people and is trying to stop the fight between the two old ladies with the clipboard.

I grab the phone that has rung about sixteen times. I say SuperLab may I help you? The man on the other end says "hey doll baby are you free for lunch?" Before I can explain that I am not Sally he starts in with graphic details about how hot she was the other day and exactly what he plans to do to her sexually when he meets her for lunch. I still cannot get a word in and am becoming very uncomfortable listening to these details. I can hear him breathing hard and I can imagine what he is doing on the other end of the phone. I say hold please as I put him on hold.

I get Sally's attention and say "personal call for you." She has finally gotten those two women settled down. She heads to the back room where we keep donuts. I figure Sally will be tied up for awhile with whoever this man is? As I get ready to call a patient a good looking man appears at the front counter asking for Sally. He has brown hair and a wedding ring matching hers so this must be the husband. I decide to be a stinker and I tell him she is in the back room to go on back. This should be interesting. I call a patient back and as we pass the back room the door is open and I can hear Sally trying to carefully end the conversation on the phone while her husband is standing there. Boy this lady has colossal nerve. Sally never seems to get rattled no matter what.

I have a man in my draw chair named Rodney Smith. He seems nice enough. Doug is drawing another male patient while talking about a fishing trip he went on recently. Doug's patient has pulled out a few pictures of fish. I can hear the phone ringing and everyone is drawing patients except Sally. Today Sally is dressed in tight white jeans, black ankle high boots and a tight white top that is quite thin and sheer. Her blonde hair is styled nice and she is wearing sparkly diamond earrings. I think the male patients enjoy looking at her. I wish she was really here to actually work. I guess she doesn't answer phones when she is occupied in the back room.

At this point I go as slow as I can and talk to my patient. I am not going to hurry so I can do all of the work in this lab. I finish up and show my patient to the bathroom, "no problem, I know the way" he assures me. He opens the door to the back room and walks right through as Sally and her husband try and separate from each other. It is hard not to laugh. As I am waiting for my patient, who is collecting his urine sample, I can see Rena and Amber. Amber is plucking her eyebrows in a draw chair and Rena is talking to the patient she is drawing about their churches and their choirs.

When the back room is free I am going to go call Liz. Why the hell not? I think, when in Rome do as the Romans do.

As my patient comes out of the bathroom he hands me his urine specimen. I will have to tell Sheryl that this place does have issues. In the past twenty minutes the phone has rang three different times, each call lasts over fifteen minutes. What must the patients think?

I see the waiting room is thinning out. I call the next patient back. As we head down the hall I hear knocking at the back door. I ask my patient to have a seat in the draw chair and I walk over to open the back door. There is no sign of Sally. She must have left with her husband. There at the door is another little old man with another dozen donuts.

I help him inside and thank him for the donuts. I offer him a seat and tell him I will go get Doug.

Doug wraps up looking at fish pictures and story sharing to go draw the man who has just brought in the donuts. I think there must be a dozen or more patients so far that are bringing donuts to the back door. I hear the centrifuge going in the processing room. Amber must have loaded it up after she finished plucking her eyebrows. I guess she does all the processing. I don't see anybody else doing it.

I go back to my poor patient who is waiting in the chair. I start getting my tubes ready and everything else set to draw her blood. This lady is a little bit irritated. She starts questioning me about why the long wait and where is the manager? Doug looks over and says "I am going on a break." She asks me if it is always this crazy busy here? I explain that I am filling in from another office but it appears to be the case. This lady has just asked me for the regional managers phone number. I oblige her and am happy to hand her Sheryls' phone number.

Apparently this is the only outpatient lab in this city. As I walk her out I check the lobby, there are only two patients waiting. Apparently the male patients that were having the card game used the end table that the magazines were on. The table is now upside down and the playing cards are all over the floor. I decide to take a picture to show Sheryl. Next I move the table back and replace the magazines on top. I see Amber sit down in the chair at the front desk. I guess that is how this office keeps going. As I am finished tidying up the Lobby I see Sally saunter into the front office.

She has a fresh cup of coffee in her hand. Boy this lady has nerve. I decide it is my turn to go to the back and call Liz.

Liz seems happy to hear from me. Apparently she is having a real hard time working with Steffy for eight hours. She says Steffy has dyed her hair green now and of course her finger nails match. This week she has green scrubs, green hair, green nails and green shoe laces. She says the patients are afraid of her and think there is seriously something wrong with her. The really old patients will not let Steffy draw their blood at all. Liz says she is calling Sheryl at lunch. Liz is telling me that Doctor Sweeney came down looking for results and asked Steffy if she needed any more green food coloring. Of course Steffy did not even understand that she was being insulted.

Liz says Dotty is doing okay but she was thirty minutes late today. Basically Liz is the only one who arrives on time, so she has to open the lab at eight a.m. She is saying she wishes she could just quit. She decides to let Steffy and Dotty draw the patients for awhile while we visit.

I am telling Liz about the male patient with the non-gestational AFP test and how they kept sending him back to the doctors office until I said something. They were clueless that there was an AFP test for men. They kept saying that he was not pregnant so it must be a mistake. Liz is now laughing her ass off. I am happy to provide her with a few laughs. Next I begin telling her all about Sally. She thinks I am making this stuff up. I assure her that I am not. So Liz says she is sick of doing all the work and that she says she is shifting into a low gear and working slower. I have been on the phone with Liz now for thirty minutes when she tells me that there are now eight people in the waiting room and the two idiots are not able to keep up. We say goodbye and agree to talk next week.

As I hang up I decide to run out to my car for a few. As I go out the back door Doug has brought the boat back with him again. Apparently he is fixing something. Doug asks if I want to make a run to the burger place? I said I guess so. I will go inside and see if anybody wants anything? Sally wants some fried zucchini and Amber wants an ice tea. There is another male patient requesting Doug.

I have the lunch money collected and everyone's order so I head out the back door and tell Doug there is a patient who has requested for him to draw his blood. He gives me his lunch order and cash and jumps out of the boat and heads inside.

 I am getting a fried zucchini. As I sit in the sun waiting for our order I am thinking these people have it made in the shade here.

Now that I have a moment to think I am trying to decide what to do about my apartment and the doggie door?

In the middle of the night Freddie Freeloader was barking his head off. As I walk out of my bedroom there is a raccoon inside the pantry helping himself to the food. I got a broom and was able to scare him off. I had trouble falling back to sleep after that. He came in through our doggie door.

Why can't I have a peaceful life? I am jolted back to the present when my order is called. I drive back to the lab with the food. Woo hoo everyone is happy to see me. Sally is on the phone up front so I take her zucchini and ranch dressing to her. I have to say it is crazy busy in the morning here but slow in the afternoons. I think the old people nap in the afternoon. As we are all gathered in the back room sharing food Sallys' name comes up. I am listening closely. "This happens all the time and has been going on for three years." Apparently she has to have a boyfriend on the side to be happy and stay married.

I miss working the front desk at Whitney Park and talking to the crazy patients. That is where the fun all begins. I also miss the fun game that Liz and I play with handing off difficult patients to the other one. I am starting to wonder if Sheryl has ever been out here to this office?

Amber opens the door to the back room asking if we see any cups of urine left in there. We all look around but don't see any. Amber starts opening cupboards in the hallway. Sure enough there are two urine cup samples on the shelf. This is what happens when you do not have a particular spot for the patients to place the samples. I wonder how long the specimens have been in there? Urine specimens need to be refrigerated after collection because bacteria can multiply rapidly. This could make it appear that the patient has bacteria in their urine when they don't. This could cause the doctor to prescribe an antibiotic for the patient when it is not needed. I seem to be the only one who is thinking about that.

It is only eleven thirty a.m. and Doug says he is taking

his lunch break. Nobody says anything even though we have all just finished eating all the food I picked up at the burger place. I wander up front and take a seat in the corner. Sally is on the phone. Probably the boyfriend. I grab a book and pretend to be interested in it while I listen in to Sally's phone call. This book lists all of the offices in all of the cities across the country with a SuperLab outpatient office. Holy smokes there are offices everywhere.

Sally is talking about a weekend escape to the mountains with someone. She must be talking to the boyfriend because she is saying Bob is acting suspicious. I am not sure why I am fascinated by this woman's antics but I am.

I am hearing children's voices. Two of Doug's children are wandering around the back. Now they have come up front. One of them has gone into Sally's private closet and opened another bag of popcorn and is alternating between eating it and throwing it at his brother.

Sally is very engaged in her conversation. Feet up on the counter, talking quietly into the phone. I decide to get up and head to the back. Doug and his girlfriend have made themselves comfortable in the boat and the little girl has the hose running and is pretending she is washing her dads truck. Rena is putting on makeup at the bathroom sink mirror. I walk in and tell her I am heading to lunch.

This town is so quiet it is scary. I decide to go for a little ride around to check it out. Other than the burger place on the corner all I am seeing are doctors offices, a hospital and a grocery store. Coming into town I did notice several billboards announcing funeral homes. I am getting homesick for my regular office and the craziness that goes with it.

Well this town is very boring so I decided not to waste

anymore gas and head back to the lab. I pull up and Doug and his girlfriend are relaxing in the sun in the boat. The little girl has now climbed into the truck and is playing around with the gadgets on the dash. I park and head inside. As I head to the front office I see nobody in the chair at the front counter. I start to walk back behind the counter and I see Sally on her hands and knees picking up popcorn. I back out of there. As I walk by the front door leading to the lobby I see the boys are tearing apart the front lobby. I cannot believe this. The boys are now jumping from chair to chair. I head to the back to call Sheryl.

"Hi Sheryl" it is Betty. "Hi there, I was wondering how you are doing out there?" she says. I ask Sheryl if she has ever been out here to this office? "Actually I haven't been out there since we signed the lease three years ago, how is it?" I said very nice. It just occurred to me while I was dialing that if I say anything negative I could end up being sent here permanently. I would not want to be here all the time. I told her that they need a table or someplace in the bathroom for the patients to put their urine specimens.

"Oh really" she says "can you fix something up while you are there?" I feel like saying you have got to be kidding me. "I will work on that" I say. "Okay let's talk again next week. I want you back at Whitney Park next week." "Okay" I say. As I hang up I realize that nobody really cares where the urine specimens are placed. I just went up front and grabbed a piece of white copy paper and wrote "urine specimens" and taped it to the outside of the cupboard where we found the specimens. There, project completed.

I laugh to myself as I walk away. I am not going to continue to do things that are way above my pay grade. Maybe I have been too conscientious? I head to the back room to call Liz. I had to hold for a bit. Finally I get Liz on the line and she sounds tired and irritated. So according to Liz Dotty is now running thirty minutes late every day and Steffy broke off another one of her claw-like finger nails and had to go have it fixed right away because she said it made her look unprofessional at her job. I laughed so hard I thought I would pee my pants. I tell Liz about the day when one of Steffys' nails came off and was stuck in the tourniquet on a patient's arm. Liz was shocked. Liz is not aware of all the crazy things that take place when she is gone.

I tell Liz all about the Sally the bimbo and her juggling two men and all that goes along with that. I was telling her all about the popcorn mess when she asked me to hold so she could take care of a problem. There was another older male patient who did not want Steffy drawing his blood.

When Liz comes back to the phone she tells me that somebody clogged up the toilet early this morning and how it was a nightmare. The patients had to use the bathroom in the lobby at Urgent Care and then walk down the hall carrying urine cups filled with urine. Apparently somebody did not have the lid screwed on right and the urine spilled out all along the carpet as they walked. Boy they aren't kidding about hospitals and medical clinics being full of germs.

Liz is now having to do everything down there including running a few tests. We agree that when I get back we should go to the casino and pool our money on dollar slot machines in the hope of winning enough money to quit our jobs.

So we visit for a little bit and then it starts getting crazy at Whitney Park and we hang up. Liz was telling me that Dotty not only shows up very late but is wearing some kind of a brace around her neck, so she is barely any help at all. I feel so sorry for Liz.

I head down the hall to see what is going on at the moment in this most interesting office? Doug has taken the girlfriend and the kids and the boat home and the waiting room looks like a tornado went through it. I am not picking it up.

It is just about time for me to head home. Tomorrow is another day. I wonder what has been going on at my apartment all day while I was gone? I wonder if Freddie Freeloader is okay?

CHAPTER

1 5

THE SUN RISES AS THE ALARM GOES OFF. I hit snooze for ten more minutes. Oh goody, another day at the nut house! As I pull up there is a different little old man standing at the back door with more donuts. Shame on Doug. As I open the door I have to take the donuts and help him inside. I am further ashamed when I hear this little old man asking Doug if the donuts are the ones he likes?

Doug is up front getting this man's paperwork done. Sally has just arrived in tight jeans, a tight top and ankle length boots. She honestly does not look like she is going to work at a lab with all geriatric patients.

Well, let's see what is happening today? I cannot believe this, nobody straightened up the lobby after Doug's kids messed it up yesterday. Our elderly patients are swerving around all the things on the floor with their walkers. Sally has started registering patients. Amber is putting her hair up in the bathroom and Rena is late. There is an old lady at the window asking Sally a bunch of questions about her tests and Sally has no idea what the answers are.

Sally is quietly sipping her coffee as she listens to the woman while looking both uninterested and not awake as she sits there. The woman is wanting to know why the doctor ordered a particular test? Of course none of us at the lab have any idea what was on the doctors mind when he ordered these tests. People in line are starting to argue amongst themselves, complaining about how hungry they are and why the damn line is not moving?

Sally is just sitting there sipping her coffee looking at the woman like she has two heads. Here comes Amber. She brings the elderly woman back and says she will see what she can do for her. Sally goes on to the next patient. Amber is like a mother hen. The elderly lady is thrilled with the personal attention. The problem is none of us are really awake at seven a.m. We are barely functioning. Luckily most of us have enough experience so we can practically draw the blood in our sleep.

I can hear two elderly women in the lobby having a rather loud political discussion. This is never a good idea. Turns out elderly people are very opinionated and very stubborn. Now an old man has yelled out that they need to shut up because they have no idea what they are talking about. I am not going out there as dealing with this type of thing is way above my pay grade. Only took me five years to realize this. Doug is sitting in the chair across from Sally reading a fishing magazine while we wait for Sally to get some patients registered.

Sally gets a personal phone call and tells them she will have to call them back. Maybe we should take bets on whether it was the husband or boyfriend?

Rena has arrived. She had a late concert last night. Honestly I need to be careful about what I say to Sheryl because these people all fit in quite well together and I do not want to work here. Maybe I should mention that Dotty would be a great fit in this office. Nobody would care if she rolls in an hour late.

Okay we are ready to roll. There are four patients requisitions done and on the counter. We each take a patient. It turns out Doug and I each get one of the two old ladies who were talking politics. Doug is looking at me like are you ready to race? I give him the look and we are off and racing. The two old ladies continue their conversation and we are going as fast as we can. Damn, the blood flowing into the tubes has slowed down and Doug has won our little game. My old lady is still talking. Well we are tied one to one. I see Sally has about eight more patients stacked up and is now on a personal call with one of her men. She is wide awake now and grinning ear to ear. Makes you wonder what is being said on the other end? I head to the counter to call another patient.

The other phone line is ringing and I keep waiting for Sally to place her man on hold and answer the phone but she never does. Holy cow. I almost cannot believe this. A couple minutes later I hear the phone ringing again, same thing. Amber comes to the back room and answers the phone. Well it is Sheryl. BUSTED! I can tell she is asking why nobody is answering the phone. Sally is still on her personal call with her feet up unaware. Amber walks to front telling Sally she has a phone call. Sally says "take a message." Amber lets her know that it's Sheryl at the main lab asking for you. Sally says goodbye to whichever one of her men she is talking to. I can hear Sally answer the phone and start making excuses for why she is not answering the phones. After drawing my patient I hear Sally telling Amber that she has to go to work at the main lab drawing blood for awhile.

Wow good for Sheryl. Now she can see what a worthless employee this woman is. This is going to be very funny. I decide to call Sheryl on my next break and tell her Dotty would be good over at this office. I cannot wait to talk to Liz. The lobby is almost empty. I am going to go call Sheryl and see what's up? It can be hard to reach Sheryl so now seems to be a good time. I tell Sheryl this was perfect timing by calling today. She tells me it is not the first time she has had this problem with Sally.

Sheryl agrees that next week I will go back to Whitney Park and Liz and I can handle the load and she will send Dotty out to replace Sally. Boy I would love to see Sally at the main lab. She will hate it. Apparently I will have Steffy in the afternoons to help me after Liz leaves. So basically I will be working alone. Sheryl asks me if there is a problem with Steffy? I say "several" and I ask her how long she has? She said one of the doctors complained saying she looked like a leprechaun last week. I was cracking up as she told me this. I ask Sheryl if there is any type of dress code here at the loonie labs? She said she honestly has never had this problem before.

I explain to Sheryl that she likes her hair and nails to match and her scrubs too, so she looks very professional. I have never heard Sheryl use such language while talking to me before. I actually feel a little sorry for Sheryl, momentarily. There I am over it. Sheryl says to see how it goes and maybe she will have to do something about Steffy. I told Sheryl how slow she is.

I am going to go to lunch and sit out in my car and contemplate my navel. I brought a protein bar and water. I cannot keep eating the hamburgers and fried zucchini. I move my car so I can have the afternoon sun on me. Now I can disrobe a little and pretend I am at the beach. I keep thinking about how I could get a better job but that takes time and money to live on while you are studying. People are not waiting in line to help me financially.

Wow! I sit in the sun for an hour. I guess I need to go back inside. I walk in the back door and all is quiet and nobody seems to care at all that I was gone or that I am back. Doug is heading out the door to go somewhere. Sally is in the bathroom reapplying makeup. I wander through the office. Very quiet.

I think I will go to the back room and see what Liz is doing at Whitney Park? The phone rings six times. I wait a few and call back. I just sit in a comfy chair behind a big desk in the back room and daydream. After my brief daydream I dial Whitney Park again and thankfully Liz answers. She tells me she was drawing a baby when I called. "So how's it going over there?" I ask. She tells me that Dotty helped hold the baby so she could draw.

Apparently Dotty had a car accident and can barely bend due to her neck hurting. Liz asked Dotty what happened and she mentioned something about swerving for a dog. Dotty has a heart of gold, but her head is up in the clouds somewhere most of the time. Poor Liz. I tell her only one more day and I will be back at Whitney Park, but our friend Sally will be at the main lab for awhile. I give Liz all the details and we agree that Dotty will have fun at that office.

Dotty just found out this morning that she has to go to the Hemlock office and according to Liz she is very angry.

Dotty hates to drive and can barely make it to Whitney Park, the Hemlock office is another thirty minutes further. My guess is she will be an hour late each day.

Liz tells me that Steffy has a beautiful new gold ring in her nose. "Oh gross" I say. "Are you messing with me?" "Nope swear to God." "Oh my God, I will never be able to look her in the eye" I say. I think this could be the last straw for me. "How are the patients handling it?" I ask. "Well a man asked her this morning if she was in the circus?" She actually said "what the hell are you talking about?" to this patient. "Seriously?" "Yep" she is starting to get a bit defensive. "Oh My" I say.

Liz tells me Cedrick is still peeing on the front of the building. We both laugh. I tell her about Doug and I having silent races while drawing the blood. She gasps and says "how the hell do you pull that one off?" So I tell her "it is easy, he just looks at me and says go with his eyes. The bigger the needle that we use, the faster the tubes fill up."

You cannot use a larger needle on patients who are on blood thinners, and I think Doug forgot that rule during one of our races earlier. His patient's arm just kept bleeding and Doug had to hold pressure for a full five minutes. The good news is it made me the winner of that crazy game.

Liz tells me that she just got back from Urgent Care for a draw on a guy that was stopped by the police for being intoxicated and the staff were placing bets on his blood alcohol level. Of course Liz got in on the bet. Fifty bucks to whoever guesses closest to the correct level. I laughed so hard tears were running down my legs. We both agreed that maybe a referral to Doctor Kevorkian would be appropriate for this patient. We wished each other a fun day tomorrow and hung up.

CHAPTER

16

WOO HOO MY LAST DAY AT THIS HEMLOCK office. I am thinking I should be fashionably late until I consider that that could get me on the shit list with Sheryl. I better try to stay on her good side. I am hurrying to get myself dressed and give my dog Freddie Freeloader food and water. I am so sick of rushing to work every damn day. I have so many more years of working it is ridiculous.

Seems like it is taking forever to get to work today.

As I drive up in the gravel behind the door to the lab I see a pathetic situation. There are two male patients with walkers on the sidewalk heading to the back door. Each one has a dozen donuts on the seat of his walker. One of them has just tipped over and there are donuts scattered all over the sidewalk. As I sit here in my car watching this scene I figure I have two choices. Back out and go around the block a few times, or go help them.

I decide instead of wasting more gas I will do the right

thing and get out of my car and help the poor elderly man on the ground. The other man is sitting on the seat of his scooter calmly holding his box of donuts. "Good morning gentlemen, how are we doing today?" No answer. I offer my hand to the man on the ground and we get him picked up and back on his walker. He is glaring at the other patient telling him this is not over. Doug finally pulls up in his car. He walks up and grabs the boxes of donuts and welcomes these two characters. He puts donuts on the desk in the back room and holds the door open for them to enter. As they enter I can see that things have not cooled down between these two men at all.

They are now pushing and shoving trying to be the first one through the doorway. This is unbelievable. Finally one just settles down in the chair and eats four donuts. The other one starts laughing saying "ha ha ha now you are not fasting and cannot get your blood drawn." The other one says "I am eighty two years old and I do not care about my cholesterol or blood sugar." Then he takes a chocolate frosted twist donut and holds it under the other guys nose and then promptly takes a huge bite and eats the whole donut in ten seconds. The other guy now walks over to the desk and tips the whole box of donuts upside down. I am thinking the doctor should have ordered a "dumbshit profile" on each of them. I tell Doug that since he started this donut game and he can deal with these two old guys.

I put my things away, find a lab coat and head up front to see what is going on? Amber is in the processing room tidying up and on the phone with her boyfriend discussing something that happened last night. Rena is in the bathroom applying makeup and Sally is in her closet fiddling with her makeup and has just unlocked the front door.

The patients are now making their way to the front counter to sign in. Looks to be about fifteen people. Two old ladies who just signed in are looking for seats while disagreeing about how hot it is going to be today. One is dressed like she lives in the snow and the other is dressed for summer. I am finding this rather amusing. Apparently the weatherman on one channel is an idiot and should never be allowed to do weather forecasts. It is hard to believe that one day I will be just like these people. I definitely do not want to live past seventy three.

These ladies are a little more civilized than the gentlemen with the donuts. I go to the back room to see how Doug is coming along? He is almost done with his patients. One is gone and the second one is discussing fishing with Doug while Doug holds pressure on his arm. I head up front to grab a requisition off the pile and call the next patient and Sally asks me if I can please see what is going on in the waiting room? Apparently Doug brought some new magazines in yesterday for our lobby. As I get closer I can see two men that are fighting over a playboy magazine.

I approach them and quietly ask them if that magazine was here in the lobby or if they brought it with them? Well apparently it was already here. I guess we now know what happens when we ask a man to bring in magazines for the waiting room. Although it is good to have magazines that appeal to both sexes I could see this becoming a problem. I quietly explain that they need to share the magazine or we will have to get rid of it.

I walk back into the front area to take a requisition off the pile and start drawing blood. I can hear Amber and Rena talking to their patients in the first room. Rena is sharing about her last concert and Amber is talking about a picnic she and her family went on. As I go to the counter to get a requisition to call the next patient I hear Sally telling somebody on the phone that she has to drive to the main lab to work. I wish I could be a fly on the wall watching her working there. She is telling the person on the other end of the phone that she has no idea why she has to go there and work.

I call the next patient back to have their blood drawn. As I bring my patient back and we walk into the drawing room we notice Doug has his fishing tackle box and everything in it spread out all over the patient exam table. He is going through his lures, like this is a perfectly normal thing for him to be doing with patients in the office. I happen to have a male patient about seventy years old who is quite fascinated with all of Doug's lures. The patient gives me his arm as he watches Doug and starts asking Doug questions about his lures while I am drawing his blood. By the time I am all finished the two of them are making a date to go fishing. It amazes me how very simple men are. There is something to be said about that.

I get labels on the tubes and give this man a urine cup and instructions on where to put it after he is done. He is still talking about going fishing with Doug. I head up to the front to see what is going on. Looks like we have a short break while we wait for Sally to get a few more patients registered. I am wondering if the patients who come here are slightly more normal than the patients in Whitney Park? It might just seem that way because I am not having to deal with them at the front desk.

Amber is working in the processing room. Rena walks up front and we chat for a few minutes. The phone rings and it is for Sally. So Rena offers to register patients while she scoots off to the back room to talk to one of her men. Doug says goodbye to his new fishing buddy as he heads to the front. He says "where's Sally?" We all say in unison "backroom."

Doug gets a piece of paper and starts taking orders for Hamburgers and fried zucchini. I cannot resist another order of zucchini and a burger as it is my last day here in this office. Doug walks right in the door to the back room without knocking and asks Sally if she wants anything from the burger place. She shakes her head no and keeps right on talking. As soon as Doug gets back she will be begging for a piece of zucchini from each of us. This lady has colossal nerve.

Well, Sally does have to watch her figure to please not only one but two men.

Rena tells me I have a phone call. Sally has tied up the back room so I take the call right in the front. It is my son wanting to know if I still want him to go to that trade school for commercial heating and air conditioning or just continue flipping burgers? I say "yes absolutely the trade school." "Well here is the thing" he says. "If I want to do it we have to go tomorrow to find out all the details and sign up. The man at the school is saving me a spot." Jeez Louise this day keeps getting better and better.

So I tell him okay. Of course I don't mind driving three hours each way tomorrow on my day off. So I tell my son to please get the apartment cleaned up and all of the dishes done and we will have to leave at seven a.m. for a ten a.m. appointment. I am fairly certain they are going to want money from me. Honestly with no child support from his father my credit is already shot. I am pretty sure nobody would loan me enough money to buy a coke.

I am considering bringing some monopoly money, but

my son would be mortified if I did that. Maybe I should bring a small tiny tree with monopoly money taped to it. What a fun fantasy that is.

The good news is that I will have my son as a captive audience for six hours tomorrow and we can discuss what his plans are with the girlfriend, who I am sure has not been taught any manners. It is really tough raising a young man, especially financially. At one point I had to start telling the creditors that if they did not stop harassing me, I would not even put their name in the hat for me to draw who would get paid next.

I want to respect my sons' privacy, but this means not barging into his bedroom. He could have several women in there for all I know. Honestly I am already tired just thinking about tomorrow's trip.

Rena has some requisitions stacked up for patients waiting to be drawn. Doug is drawing and so is Amber. Frankly I am so thankful today is my last day. Sally is getting on my very last nerve. As I head towards the counter to pick up a requisition I hear Amber call for help. Her patient has collapsed on the floor. I ask Rena to dial nine one one as I head into the room. Amber is trying to see if the woman has just passed out or if it is something more serious. We get a pillow off the bed in Dougs' room and try to make her comfortable. Okay, Amber will stay with her. She is breathing. I close the door so I can keep the line moving without somebody seeing this patient on the ground and call the next patient. So now we only have two draw chairs in the back room that we can use.

Just as I am heading down the hall the fire department and paramedics are arriving. They come in the back door. This keeps things flowing and helps keep the patients in the lobby calm and unaware. We don't need to get everyone upset and asking a bunch of questions. Due to privacy laws we cannot tell them anything.

Sally passes me in the hall asking what is going on? Nobody answers her. We all just keep doing what we are doing. Sally looks a bit concerned. She is probably most concerned because she knows she is a royal screw up and has not been doing her job lately. Sally ends up just walking out of the room, because she is unable to answer any of the firemen and paramedics questions.

I bring my patient to the back draw room. Her name is Mary. She seems nice enough but she keeps saying okay after each sentence. As I am getting out the alcohol and getting the needle ready she yells loudly "what is going on in here?" I turn around as the emergency responders are wheeling the patient down the hall past our door. I try to give her a simple explanation and simply tell her that a patient collapsed and we had to call 911. I am hoping this explanation is enough for her but fearing deep down that it will not be. Lovely, now I have to answer more questions before we can proceed with the blood draw.

This lady wants to know all the details, but due to privacy laws we cannot give this woman any information about another patient. I am trying to put myself in my patient's shoes. If they told me a patient collapsed and we had to call nine one one I would say okay. What am I missing here? I am wondering if all the questions stem from just being old and bored or what? Alright the back door has closed and hopefully we can now get back to blood drawing.

I am so anxious to get back to my office in Whitney park?

I miss hearing Liz say "see ya wouldn't want to be ya" as she leaves every day. I also miss our Scrabble game. I know Liz misses having another phlebotomist with lots of experience. She told me in our last conversation that she is spending all her time redrawing patients that Steffy and Dotty miss.

I am just about finished drawing my patients blood and holding pressure on her arm for a couple minutes. With geriatric patients you really have to hold the pressure on their arm yourself because although you tell them they frequently do not use any pressure at all. It can look like they might be putting pressure but they really aren't. Then they come back with blood running down their arm and that really freaks them out.

When you are on your last day someplace and anxious to be gone the time just seems to drags on. That is what is happening today. I open the back door to see Doug backing his boat in. He is dragging fishing poles out to get them ready for a fishing trip. I walk up front to see who is doing what? Sally is having a cup of tea and eating popcorn while she talks on the phone. I turn around and say "going to lunch" to Amber who is in the processing room as I walk out. Screw it I am taking an hour and a half. I move my car across the lot so it faces the sun and take my scrubs off. I have shorts and a tank top underneath. I will pretend I am at the beach. I can see Doug playing with his fishing stuff. This is absolutely hilarious. Work four hours and get paid for eight.

I am pretty sure Sally did not hear me say that I was going to lunch. Oh well. I think I will call Liz when I go back in and then it should be time for me to leave. Wow, the sun feels amazing. I have a camping chair I am relaxing in. Boy time sure does fly when you are at the beach. Well I guess I should get my scrubs back on just in case I actually have to draw someone's blood before I leave. I walk in the back door and put my stuff in a cupboard.

I am heading down the hall to the front to just make sure everyone sees me and knows that I did come back from lunch. As I settle into the chair at the big desk in the back the door opens and it is Sally's boyfriend who looks to be twelve years old. He sticks his head in the door asking for her. I tell him that she is up front, go on in. Now wouldn't it be hilarious if her husband showed up right now? Wow what a riot, I just realized that I am in their spot. I dial Liz at the lab. She hears my voice and laughs and says "hang on, going to the back."

As Liz comes on the line she sounds exhausted. She says she is ready for the loony bin. She tells me that the patients have been asking if you quit? "Oh really?" I say. She says "I told them you will be back next week." Liz is telling me about her week from hell. Apparently she has been alone all week with Steffy. Dotty had to take time off because she can't turn her head. Her neck is still hurting from her car accident.

Liz tells me that this has been the worst day ever. Steffy arrived for her nine a.m. shift at ten forty five a.m. because one of her nails broke, and she had to have it fixed before she could come to work because she has to look professional at all times. I really do not think Steffy's elevator goes all the way to the top. Liz tells me how bad she wanted to slap Steffy up alongside the head. I remind Liz that Steffy did the exact same thing to me and used the same damn excuse. Liz says she needs a beach day as soon as I am back. So I ask if everything else going okay? "Hell no" she says. So Liz proceeds to tell me that Cedrick was out front doing his usual peeing on the front of the building this morning when he got his pubic hair caught in his zipper and was screaming for help until the fire department got there. Apparently he drew quite a crowd.

She said she could see him rolling around on the ground in pain and creating a major scene in front of the doors at the front of the Whitney Park Health Center. After I finish laughing hysterically I tell her that I had discovered him not wearing underwear a couple months ago when he forgot to close his fly. Liz said she wants to quit this miserable job but cannot afford to right now. I said I was in the same boat.

We made a pact that we would both start playing the lottery religiously and whoever wins the lottery first will give the other one enough to retire early. Then we realize how ridiculous that sounds because we have already been playing for a million years so far and nothing! I tell her I think we should start sharing some dollar slot machines at the casino and share the winnings. She agrees, so next week should be lots more fun. I continue to tell her about the two old men fighting over being the first one in the door with donuts in their hands and the whole sordid story. At least I got a chuckle out of her. Liz is telling me that the health center has been getting crazy busy lately. This news is enough to make me quit right now.

I have to say I am really looking forward to another beach day with Liz real soon. She says she is too. Liz asks me if I can get a picture of Sally before I go? She thinks it would be nice to put a face with a name. So I say I will snap the picture and I will see her next week.

I open the door to the back room and head down the hall to see what is going on in the front office. Sally is doing something in her little room off the front office. Rena is stocking her draw station and Amber is sitting in one of the draw chairs eating a snack talking to Rena. It just dawns on me that Doug is gone. I guess I will go sit in a chair up front and see if I can eavesdrop on Sally's phone calls. Sally sees me and mumbles hello. Next thing I know Sally is on the phone again. Feet up. I think that is a sign it is time for me to snap picture. Getting her in her usual pose will be great.

I pick up a magazine to thumb through so she won't think I am just there to listen in. Sally asks me what it is like at the main lab? Looks like I have a dilemma. Do I make it sound wonderful or make it sound awful? I tell her that it opens at seven a.m. and that it is nonstop until two p.m. Then busy again from four to six p.m. She gasps at the idea of actually working, until six p.m. and then having to deal with an hour drive home. I suggest she call Sheryl to find out what her hours will be? I cannot believe it is Friday afternoon and she has no idea what her hours are on Monday.

I should call the main lab and tell Bill to take her with him to the mental health unit when he goes. You know that old saying *You reap what you sow*. Well she has it coming if you ask me. I am wondering how long Sheryl intends to keep her there? I am dialing Bill. This will be so funny.

I tell Sally that there are two draw stations in the hallway where she may be drawing blood and it is right outside Sheryl's door. I tell her that it is very cramped in there compared to this office. She looks more and more depressed as I explain what it is like. No extra rooms or private areas for talking on the phone. I tell her that if it is not busy you have to find something to do to look busy.

Well it is almost time for me to head out. Doug walks in and chats with Sally for a few. He says he was at the bait shop getting bait for his early morning fishing trip tomorrow morning. I tell them all that it was fun working here and that I would see them again. Woo hoo, back to my own crazy office. I say goodbye to Rena and Amber on my way out.

CHAPTER

SIX A.M. ALREADY? NO FREAKING WAY. I push snooze. I was having a great dream. I was in the Bahamas playing in the water and sipping cocktails. "Oh no" I say to myself as I stumble out of bed to the shower. Why couldn't it be real? I have to hurry now and shower and dress and take care of feeding Freddie Freeloader. I am starving. I can't be late. If I really hurry I can stop at the donut shop and get a jumbo coffee. I leave my son a note asking him to please take Freddie Freeloader out for a walk.

Shoot, I have to stop and put ten dollars of gas in my car. I wish I would have done that on my way home Friday. Why do I put things off? Maybe I can pull into the station by the lab and get coffee and donut there to save time. The thought of dealing with the patients with no coffee or food makes me cringe.

I hate to admit it but I have gotten used to having a few extra minutes in the morning at the other office before facing the patients. That is one of the drawbacks of the Whitney Park office. I have to open the lab on time because many of the patients are fasting and they all feel like they must eat something immediately. It amazes me that the patients do not seem to realize that they could come in at eight forty five a.m. and have little to no wait. When they arrive just as we open they end up just waiting in line until it is their turn.

As I pull into the Whitney Park Health Center I see an ambulance parked at the back of the Urgent Care Center. That might mean that will I have to go down there to do a STAT draw which means it takes precedence over everything else. That will make for some mighty unhappy patients in our waiting room. Hopefully I can get some patients drawn before Urgent Care calls. As soon as Liz comes at eight thirty a.m. then we will be alright. As I head down the hallway to the lab I see we already have eight people in line. Each one is feeling like they will starve to death if they do not eat in the next fifteen minutes.

I recognize a few of the patients, but it also looks like we have a few new ones. I see we have two old ladies talking nasty to one another in the front of the line. One lady brought a bunch of food to eat after her blood draw while she is waiting to be picked up. The other one is telling her that she cannot be sitting in a waiting room full of starving people eating her food. She tells her if you want to die today just try it.

"Okay ladies please sign in and have a seat, and let's try to be polite to one other" I say. The one lady who is pretty small says that some people are too stupid. Then she looks at the other lady and says "you don't really plan on eating all that food do you?" The larger woman looks her right in the eye and says "watch me."

I am starting to think that *too stupid to live* should be a diagnosis. So now it looks like all of the patients have all signed in. I am starting to call them up to the window to make sure they are fasting and to get their insurance information.

I see Mrs. Stevens is out there and no damn way am I in the mood for her. I am definitely putting Liz's name on her requisition. That will be my happy Monday and happy to be back gift to her. I call Mary Johnson up to the window. She says "oh thank God you came back. We thought you might have gotten fired or quit." I just smile and say "no I am still here." I ask her how things went while I was gone? She tells me that this is her third time to come in because she could not stand to wait in the long line. She said Liz was cranky with that weird looking young girl who is trying to learn how to draw blood. I think to myself, wow it must have been really bad?

Liz should be here in ten minutes. I call Mrs. Stevens up to the window and she starts in immediately. "Honey how long do you think it will be until you get to me?" I tell her it is hard to guess but Liz will be here soon and then it will go faster. "Can you tell what the doctor is looking for?" "No, I have no idea" I say as I look at her requisition. "Well I think I had a heart attack maybe two weeks ago, but the pain eventually got better and I am still alive so I guess I am fine?" She then tells me how nauseated she is most of the time and asks if I know why that is? I repeat same answer as before.

Liz has just arrived and immediately goes into the break room and I can hear her setting up the Scrabble game. So I thank Mrs. Stevens and I grab a little sticky note and put Liz's name on it and snicker to myself as I put it in the stack.

Liz walks out of the break room and says "thank God

you finally came back, this place is a shit magnet." Then as an after thought she says "when you get a chance can you *check the specimen*?" "Okay" I say.

Looks like everyone is registered and we are ready. I quickly pick up the first requisition off the pile so Liz will get Mrs. Stevens. I am happy to be back. I have my patient in my chair in front and can hear Liz calling Mrs. Stevens back. She has already starting talking about her ailments and they have not even reached the back room yet. Liz is looking irritated. As she gets to the doorway to her room, which is right across from where I am sitting, she says "hey Bett" as I look over and she gives me the finger as she walks in her room. I laugh out loud.

As I call my next patient I see Steffy walking in. Oh no, she has bright red hair and nails that match. I say loudly "hello Steffy" so Liz will know that she is here. "What happened to your hair?" I ask. "Oh my mom gave me some money for my birthday and I treated myself to a new hairdo" she says. My other style was looking old and unprofessional. This time she has her hair spiked up on top. This color of red is by no means a natural red color and I also notice her new nose ring, lovely. Today she has on red flip flops. Geez Louise she looks like a five year old who dressed herself. As I look closer she has some kind of red rouge on her cheeks. Good grief this is really bad, just wait till Liz sees this.

I finish drawing this patient's blood and after I take it to the back I am going to sneak into the back room and *check the specimen*. Damn that Liz, she just started this Scrabble game out using all seven tiles which gives her a huge score. Now I am going to have to really work to catch up. It is taking me awhile to figure out a decent word.

As I walk out of the back room I hear Liz telling Steffy that she cannot work in flip flops and she must go home and come back with some type of closed toe shoe. I am so thankful Liz said something. So Steffy is walking out the door ten minutes after she walked in. I remind her on her way out to make sure and fix her time card to reflect hours actually worked. I actually spelled it out when I saw her blank face. "You are not getting paid when you are not here in the lab." Out the door she goes.

As Liz walks out of the processing room I say "when you get a chance can you *check the specimen*?" She laughs and says I am fairly sure you did not catch up to me.

I ask Liz how long Steffy has been wearing the bright red stuff on her cheeks? Liz is telling me today is the first time, she thinks it must have something to do with the red hair. I need to find out if Sheryl is aware that we have an employee who looks like a hooker.

While the centrifuge is going Liz and I are talking about how long she thinks we need to wait after me coming back before we take another mental health day? Liz says she is getting desperate for a trip to the beach to clear her head. Sounds like she had lots of headaches while I was gone. Thirty minutes later here comes Steffy again. She is wearing red high heels this time. I think we will send her down to Urgent Care and Primary Care all afternoon to impress upon her that high heels are a bad choice when your job requires you to be on your feet all day. By five p.m. she will barely be able to walk. We should get a pool going with bets on whether she even will put two and two together enough and wear walking shoes tomorrow.

Just the thought of Steffy hobbling up and down the hall in these heels makes me laugh. I tell Liz my idea and she loves it. So it's a plan.

Liz is heading to the back room to *check the specimen* in our ongoing scrabble game. Damn that Liz she is really kicking my ass in this game. I hope to catch up at my next turn. I am registering a patient at the front desk and Steffy is standing at the counter. Both phone lines start ringing. I put one on hold and answer the other. It is Jackie down in Urgent Care. They need blood drawn. I tell her we will be down. I tell Steffy there is a draw and can she please do it?

She gives me her I'm exhausted exhale before grabbing a kit and gloves. I grab the other line. I answer and I hear a young man on the other end. He starts in with a story about his wife demanding he do this test. I am hoping he gets to the point quickly. He finally gets to the point, he needs a semen analysis. This requires him to come into the lab and collect his semen in a cup. He is asking me if we have a private room with a bed and soft lighting and pornographic movies? This is definitely a Liz call. She is still in the back at the scrabble game. I excuse myself from the patient standing at the window and go to the break room to tell Liz that there is a phone call for her. "Line 1, I think it might be your son" I say as I go back to registering my patient. I hear her answer the phone in the back room and think gotcha again. I cannot help laughing.

This young man is in for a huge reality check. I am not sure where on earth he got the idea that the laboratory had special accommodations for him? All we have is a urine cup labeled with his name and a bathroom with a door that hopefully locks. Liz is going to really get me good for this one. Seriously, fifteen minutes later she is still on the line with this guy. I hear her say no that will not work. She is leaning around the corner as far as the cord will go making mean faces at me. I write a note on a piece of paper saying "you could offer to help him." Now she is giving me the finger, as I am doubled over laughing.

Boy, am I glad to be back at this office. These little games we play make the day go by faster.

I call my patient back to my draw chair in the front office. I don't want to miss the look on Liz's face when she hangs up. Finally I can tell she is about to hang up then I hear her say "excuse me?" Geez another question? She is having all the fun! I hear her say "only if the hotel is next door to our office." I am looking out the window and nope, no hotel. This is utterly ridiculous. I am starting to wonder if this is a prank call? I hear her say "look, figure it out I have to go" and she hangs up the phone. As she walks out she sticks her tongue out at me. Poor Liz. She will definitely be paying me back for this one. I will give her a few minutes to cool down and then ask her all about it.

Nobody could ever say this job is boring. I call the main lab to have them send a courier for the STAT that Steffy is supposed to be drawing. She has been down there awhile. I call the next patient up to the window. Mrs. Weinstein. This woman is a huge whiner. If I had not just given Liz a doozy I would put her name on the requisition as if this lady request-ed her. I don't think Liz can handle another problem patient until tomorrow.

Mrs. Weinstein begins telling me how she went to the main lab and nobody there could get my blood, so they sent me here. "Oh really" I say. "They seem to have all kids work-ing over there" she adds. I tell her that next time she needs to ask for Bill "he is way better than I am." This is another fun game we play. Bill will be so frustrated smoke will be coming out of his ears. We tell patients that so and so over at the main lab is the best and to ask for that person by name. That is how I will get back at Bill for repeatedly locking me in the closet.

"Well I think this lab should reimburse me for my gas for the long drive over here." I let her know that I could call Sheryl and ask if she would like. "I hit every damn light on red" Mrs. Weinstein continues. "Oh that must make it feel farther, but I know it is less than 10 miles" I tell her. "Oh really? Well I guess that is not that far."

I excuse myself to answer the phone. It is Steffy asking me to come down to Urgent Care. I ask if Liz will do it and she says "no way."

I tell her I will come down after I finish with Mrs. Weinstein. So I bring Mrs. Weinstein back to my draw chair. Her arm is full of holes, all of the best veins have been used. I find a tiny vein and manage to get enough blood with a small three cc syringe. As I draw her blood she is telling me about a problem with her doctors nurse but honestly I could not tell you even one single word she said. "Okay leave the tape on for a little while" I tell her. She gets up and waddles out to the waiting room mumbling something. I am grabbing my draw kit, and gloves and I tell Liz I am heading down to Urgent Care. She looks upset so I give her a hug and assure her that we will do a mental health day real soon.

"Oh my" I say as I look for Steffy down in Urgent Care. All their exam rooms are full and then I see a trail of blood drops that lead me to Steffy. I almost feel bad for her as she stands there in those crazy tall heels. I ask her to follow me outside so we can talk freely. This patient appears to be in his sixties and is lying on his stomach with a coke bottle sticking out of his rectum. Steffy has no idea how to get his blood with him lying on his stomach. I tell her to just watch and learn. I get a small butterfly needle and put in on a syringe and get the blood from the back of his arm between the wrist and the elbow. This patient looks to be asleep so I just check his hospital ID bracelet and try not to wake him.

Steffy and I walk back to the lab to get the blood ready for the courier. I get the blood spinning in the centrifuge. Steffy has answered the phone and is listening intently but not responding. She places somebody on hold. "The nurse is saying that they need the blood down at Urgent Care because the patient is being transferred to ECU." "What is ECU?" Steffy asks. "ECU generally means Eternal Care Unit." Sounds similar to ICU.

The Staff uses this term so that nearby patients don't know what is going on and to let the office staff know that the patient has died or expired. This sounds more professional. Sounds like the poor man may have died. I pick up the phone to confirm. Yes, that is it. So I ask Steffy to please go stop the centrifuge and gather his blood and place it in a specimen bag and take it back down there. I see she can barely walk and I find it hard not to feel sorry for her. Hopefully this lesson will stick in her mind. She looks miserable as she heads down the hall. I take a seat in my draw chair as Liz is in the chair at the front window.

This gives us a few minutes to talk. Liz really needs a mental health day badly, we agree to go to the beach this Friday. This perks her up again. So we are talking about whether we are going to get fish and chips and then go to the beach or bring sandwiches? I tell her that we need to send Steffy down to Urgent Care to do all of the draws because she needs more practice drawing in different situations. I told her about the poor guy down in Urgent Care. "Seriously. Is it a full moon?" Liz says. So Liz and I visit for a few minutes while Steffy is gone.

"I better get going to lunch so you can head home" I tell Liz. I think I will just sit in my car today and eat. I see the coroner van is parked at the back of Urgent Care. I am parked under a shade tree in the employee parking lot. It feels nice to just sit and daydream and observe people.

People watching at the Whitney Park Health Center can be quite interesting. A couple of boys are tossing a football back and forth on the lawn. I am wondering if we can get away with another beach trip?

As I walk back into the lab Liz is gathering her things and getting ready to leave. I tell her that we should plan on this Friday for the beach. Liz heads to the door and says "see ya wouldn't want to be ya" as she walks out the door.

CHAPTER

1 8

I AM GOING INTO THE BACK ROOM to *check the specimen*. Steffy is sitting at the front desk. I wonder if we should put her up there to scare the patients off. I am taking my time taking my turn at Scrabble and I need to do one great word so I can catch up with Liz. After about twenty five minutes I decide that I had better go see what Steffy is up to? There are two older men at the counter. Actually I know who these two characters are.

These are the two clowns who were both riding on the same scooter that crashed into our front window. One of them is saying to the other one "see, I told you so. It is her after all." Apparently they have a bet going on whether Steffy is the same girl they saw in the circus the last time it was in town? Now, if I were in her shoes I would be embarrassed and ashamed, but that does not seem to be the case here. She is laughing and carrying on with them. She does not appear to be one of the sharpest tools in the shed. I ask them where their scooter was and the bigger one says "his wife took the scooter away" as he points to his friend.

Unbelievable. Steffy actually seems to be having fun talking to these two. I walk up and asked if everything is okay? "Yes, I am just visiting with our patients here" she says. "Can you believe it? They actually thought that I was the same lady who worked in the circus?" "You don't say" I say. I head over to the printer to pull some results and walk them down to Primary Care, while she visits with her new friends. After I give Primary Care the results I grab a few magazines, mostly out of habit. I think I will take a seat in the far corner of the lobby here and stay gone from the office for a few.

Wait until I tell Liz about this. Liz has zero patience with Steffy right now after having to spend every afternoon with her. Liz thinks that there is most definitely something wrong with her.

I need to call Dotty out at the Hemlock office in a few days and see what she thinks of that office. Poor Dotty. I am sure she is hating the drive. She can barely stand to drive the fifteen minutes to this office. I bet she is running thirty to forty minutes late everyday.

Well it has been thirty minutes so I guess I better head back down to our lovely office. What a surprise, Steffy still has one of those guys in her draw chair. Who takes thirty minutes to draw blood from two people? Just saying.

I check the processing room and it looks like we are caught up. Yippee! I settle into the chair at the front counter and the phone rings. It is Jackie in Urgent Care. There is a draw at Urgent Care and I tell her Steffy will be right down. I go to the doorway and tell Steffy there is a draw in Urgent Care and I need her to go do it. She looks to be hobbling to the processing room with the blood she has just drawn from her two new friends. Let's see what type of shoes she picks to wear tomorrow? Boy it feels good to relax. I think I will call Dotty and see how it is going.

"Hi Dotty it's Betty. How goes it?" She is in the front and can't really talk. I tell her to check in from the phone in the back room when she can. Poor Dotty. I wonder what she thinks of the Hemlock office? I would love to be a fly on the wall over there right now. I can just picture the donut game getting out of control and Doug doing few draws. Unfortunately Dotty will have no information on Sally as she is at the main lab. Maybe I can arrange to go have lunch with Bill one day and get all the dirt on Sally. Knowing Bill he will be attracted to her so I will have to be careful what I say.

The phone rings and it is Steffy calling from the Urgent Care Center. She says the doctor wants something called blood cultures ordered. She says it says x two and she has no idea what that means? I am feeling myself getting irritated. I tell Steffy to bring her kit and return to the lab. This is pissing me off. They are not paying me enough money to have to train these young phlebotomists. Blood cultures are a special test usually ordered when there is a fever of unknown origin.

You have to put a certain amount of blood into individual bottles and they have to have several more things done in Microbiology. One of the bottles is aerobic, and the other one is anaerobic (without Air). This part is dealt with in Microbiology at the hospital or lab. They also have certain specific steps you must follow during the collection process. If you do not follow the correct procedures the results will not be accurate. Damn it, now I have to go do the blood culture collection in Urgent Care and I have to bring the little nit wit with me.

Steffy should have never been sent here to work without this basic knowledge. It amazes me how quickly my mood can go from awesome to pissed off.

Well here is the little darling right now, as Steffy comes hobbling through the door in her heels carrying her lab kit. I get my kit out and make sure I have everything I need. I begin to explain the procedure to Steffy and show her exactly what she needs to draw for blood cultures x two.

I am explaining that the x two means two sets of blood cultures, which equals four bottles. I am trying to explain to Steffy that she needs to make sure one bottle is aerobic and the other is anaerobic, the bottles are clearly labeled. You also need a special scrub brush kit to clean the patient's arm for each blood culture. So we need at least two cleaning towelettes. I tell her to grab eight towelettes because she may miss the vein and have to start fresh again.

I will walk her through the entire procedure because she needs to learn how to do this. I am getting a freaking headache just thinking about it.

You have to draw the blood from different sites about ten minutes apart. This is most likely going to generate phone calls from Sheryl since we have to put the phones on hold and there will be nobody in the office until we get back from this ordeal. Bottom line is the office will have nobody at the desk for at least thirty minutes, depending on how well the phlebotomist collecting the specimen does, and it could easily be as long as forty five minutes. This is an example of when having a phlebotomist with lots of patience is helpful.

It is kind of comical watching Steffy trying to put the glass bottles for blood cultures into her kit and not having enough room. This also means additional weight on her very sore feet and two more trips down the hall. I am actually laughing. I kind of thought I was laughing to myself until she asked me what was so funny? Oops! So we head down the hall to the Urgent Care together. I should be paid more for training people. I need to seriously win the lottery.

We arrive at the patient's bedside. I watch as Steffy checks the patient's ID bracelet. I am walking her through this procedure and our patient is looking a bit nervous with this bizarre looking phlebotomist, nose ring and all, learning how to do this particular test. When Steffy finds the vein she is going to use I explain to her that the scrubbing of the arm is done in a circular motion from the inside of the circle out. She starts to ask me why and then after seeing the look on my face she just closes her mouth. I explain that after the arm dries she will clean it one more time with betadine the same way. Also I tell her that she cannot touch the arm again to feel for the vein because she would contaminate the site.

I can see this is going to be an issue because she took her eyes off the spot. In my mind I am in Hawaii on a boogie board playing in the water, and a tan shirtless young man has just arrived with a snack and a cocktail. This is helping me get through this ordeal nicely. Meanwhile Steffy is doing the draws for the blood cultures.

She has gotten the first one done and now we wait a few minutes while she looks for a spot to do the second draw. Well the young man in my mind has just motioned me over to the cabana. Whew this is just what the doctor ordered. It must have taken about five minutes before I realized Steffy is trying to get my attention. Oops, my bad! Back to reality.

Steffy is looking for another spot for the next draw. At

the same time I am looking for a chair to sit down and relax in. Awww that's better. Okay Steffy has finally got the blood and is putting the blood into the blood culture bottles and labeling the bottles with the proper information. Ten more minutes and we are ready to head back to the lab.

When we return to our lab Steffy is surprised to see about ten angry patients sitting in the waiting room. "What is going on here?" says one woman in a nasty tone. I let her know that we had to go to Urgent Care to draw some blood. More patients are chiming in with their own nasty comments. I am not explaining it to them again.

Another beach day is definitely in order for Liz and I very soon.

"Has everyone signed in?" I ask. "What the hell difference does it make if nobody is here in the office?" says a man in a loud voice. Good point I think. I call the first patient listed on the clipboard. There is no answer so I go on to the next one. If this man never signed in then he will be last. I call Mrs. Brown to the front. As she starts speaking I remember her last visit here and think here we go again.

"Honey I need to talk to you" she says. "Well okay ma'am" I say. She proceeds to tell me that she does not want the girl with the colored hair and crazy thing in her nose to draw her blood. So I tell her I need to register the other patients and then I can draw her blood. She sits down and waits patiently. Steffy can start drawing now, so I call the next patient up to the window. Mr. Switzer hands me a requisition for lab tests. As I look at the tests I realize these are fasting tests.

Crap, he is going to blow a fuse when I tell him he needs to come in first thing in the morning, before breakfast. "Sir I am sorry to inform you that these tests require fasting." "Are you kidding me?" he says. "No sir." I explain what he needs to do. He says "I want to talk to a supervisor right now." I wrote Sheryls' phone number on the top of his requisition and hand it back to him.

He slams the door so hard I thought the glass would break. Honestly who could blame him for being mad? Okay, I call Mrs. Brown back and I thank her for waiting. I see Steffy is drawing at her usual snails pace. "So Mrs. Brown how are you today?" I ask her. "Honey I really don't know what I am going to do with Marty? He went fishing with his friend Fred Watkins and I came home from shopping to find him cleaning fish on my kitchen counter. The kitchen smells so bad I don't know how I will ever get rid of that smell?"

"Oh that sounds gross" I say. "That's not all, this morning he forgot to put the lid on the blender and I have some kind of green slime all over my damn walls in the kitchen. I am afraid I will have to just shoot him one night while he is asleep." "Oh my, you don't really want to do that do you?" I ask. "Yes I do. I am sick of him. I have been cleaning up after him for forty two years. He is a Beast. Maybe I will shoot his family jewels off. Do you have any idea what type of gun would be easy for my small hands to use? I think I will need to shoot him at least ten times to make sure he is really dead."

Geez this is actually a first, I am getting the feeling she has no friends and I am her only person to talk this over with. "Are you sure you want to use a gun? That could be messy. Would you still want to live in the house after he is dead?" "Of course I want to live in the house after I kill him" she says. "That is the whole reason I want to kill him, so some people will come and remove him from my house. I am going to redecorate the whole house with the life insurance money."

"Ma'am, do you have any kids that you could talk to about this problem?" I ask. "My daughter is around and she hates him too" she says. "Maybe could you go stay with your daughter for a while" I suggest. Her brow wrinkles and I can tell she is thinking. "You know that's a great idea. I am going to pack after he goes to sleep and be gone before he wakes up. But if I get home and he has not cleaned the kitchen I may have to kill him before I leave."

"Mrs. Brown, that is a bad idea because then you will be in prison and he will for sure ruin your house." "Yes, I think you are right Dear" she says after thinking about it for a minute or two. I can tell that she is trying to think of another idea when she says "maybe I could sell him to some lucky woman, do you think anyone would want to buy him? I am thinking of having an auction." After thinking some more she says "crap, nobody is going to pay money for him with a one inch penis."

At this point I am grinning ear to ear. "Honey do you think it would be easier and cheaper if I just poison him? That is less messy right?" she is now asking me. Oh my, I really need to get this conversation going in a different direction. "Mrs. Brown I think you need to take a little time and think this over a little more."

I am honestly surprised at the degree of hate this elderly woman seems to have for her husband. I finish drawing her blood and while I am taping her arm she is sharing a few other ideas and feelings about how she plans to kill him.

At this point I am wondering if I should report this to someone, but normally Mrs. Brown is a pretty nice lady and her husband has always been a pain in the ass when he comes to the lab. Honestly I wouldn't mind not having to deal with him anymore either since I already have my hands full with crazy old male patients. I think Cedrik gets first place. This urinating on the front of the building is a bit crazy.

I follow Mrs. Brown out to the front and tell her to have a nice day and let me know how she is doing? She says she will and gives me a wink. I guess I am her buddy.

Wow Steffy is still on her first patient and I took a really long time with my last patient. I am going to tippy toe back and see if I can peek without her seeing me and see what is taking so long? Holy cow! Steffy is giving this male patient a massage on the exam table in the room. What to do about this? This has never happened before. I walk into the room and Steffy looks up and says "oh hi there." I tell Steffy that I need to talk with her in the back room. I hear her excuse herself and follow me out. I can hear the old man yelling, "hey, where are you going?" When I close the door I ask Steffy to please explain to me what the hell she is doing?

"Well as I was checking for veins he told me about the pain in his back and I thought maybe I could practice my massage technique on him? I am actually planning on becoming a massage therapist in the future. He says I am really good." "Steffy, this is a medical lab and our job is to draw blood from the patients and nothing more. This is inappropriate on so many levels and I am going to have to report this to Sheryl" I tell her. "That's fine with me" Steffy continues, "I am very proud of my skills. I wonder if Sheryl would sell me this table at a great price?"

Seriously? Steffy looks so proud. I honestly feel like I am for sure in the Twilight Zone.

Steffy tells me "I am thinking this job is really not my kind of job anyhow." I say to myself do ya think? Steffy proceeds to tell me "I mean I like being a medical professional and looking so professional in my outfits and I would kind of miss that part." I am struggling to keep a straight face and am thinking her elevator definitely does not go to the top floor.

Boy our new generation of workers are really something.

I explain to Steffy that she needs to get that patient out of the office and get busy drawing blood, and it should take her no more than five minutes with each patient.

Steffy gasps and says "wow I am not sure if I can go that fast?" I tell her she had better get it done. Steffy says "wow you are kind of being mean to me today. I am feeling very scared and unsafe right now. I think I need a quiet place to regroup right now." I tell her that if she doesn't get busy working like the professional that she believes she is, she will be fired and then she will have twenty four hours a day to enjoy a quiet space.

Suck it up sister. Steffy says she is going to talk to Sheryl about the way I have been treating her. I agree that that is a good idea. Make sure you tell Sheryl that you are feeling scared and unsafe and need a quiet place to regroup. I am trying not to laugh. I am wondering if this just me or if this a most ridiculous conversation among medical professionals. Maybe Sheryl will be able to see what I have been dealing with.

I tell Steffy "I want you to register the next four patients and immediately start drawing as soon as you have the last one registered." I head to the back room where all the machines for running lab tests are kept. I pull up a chair to call Sheryl. What the hell is going on? A quiet place to regroup? Really? These kids are in another world. Does she not realize what her life would be like if she loses the job? Maybe she lives with her parents? I was married with a two year old at her age. This girls only responsibility is getting to work on time in decent attire. Maybe Sheryl will either fire her or keep her at the main lab for awhile. I have to tell you this girl has gotten on my very last nerve.

Sheryl comes on the phone and says "hey Betty, whats up?" "Well Sheryl, I just discovered Steffy giving a male patient a massage on the exam table with his shirt off." "What the hell?" she says. I explain to Sheryl what I told Steffy to do and how Steffy felt I was being mean to her and that she needed a quiet place to regroup. "Did she find a quiet space?" Sheryl asks? "Hell no" I reply. I tell Sheryl that Steffy is up front registering patients and I fill her in on everything I told her.

"Okay keep me informed and tell her to stop by my office right after work, and let her know that if it takes her longer than thirty minutes to arrive she is fired." "Will do" I said. We hang up.

Working with Steffy feels more like I am babysitting my son or one of his friends. Frankly, I had hoped that coming to work would be a break from the kids. I hate to admit it but I wish I had a different job and maybe I should have gone onto nursing. So I walk out and Steffy is drawing. I call a patient back so we can clear out the waiting room and then I can relay Sheryl's message to Steffy. Luckily I have an easy patient to draw right now and then hopefully a short break.

Steffy and I meet up in the processing room with our paperwork and blood samples. I give her the message from Sheryl. Steffy says "why is this such a big deal? I was just helping the patient. That message from Sheryl sounds pretty threatening." I try not to laugh. I wonder what this girls' story is? She seems to have no experience in the real world.

I am just about caught up on the processing and we have fifteen minutes until we close. I ask Steffy to grab the results off the printer and run them down to Primary Care. She looks at me and looks at the clock and is practically running down the hall in her high heels. What an Image this is! Okay the courier is here and this delightful day is almost over. I tell Steffy to go ahead and go because I know what parking is like at the main lab.

I can just picture Steffy hurrying in her car. Next I am picturing her hurrying to find a space to park and trying to walk six blocks to the main lab at the end of the day in her heels. I guess not everyone can be smart and well organized and for sure there is no shortage of stupid people. I feel grateful to be one of the smart people. I must remember to share this incident with Liz in the morning. I will also tell her about my new friend, Mrs. Brown.

Finally the day is over. I am going to get some Chinese food on my way home for dinner. As I pull up to my apartment my neighbor beneath me is walking over to chat. She is asking if I would let her take Freddie Freeloader to a nice family in the mountains?

After some thought I am in agreement. I want him to have a wonderful home and I am no longer able to provide that for him. He is a wonderful sweet dog and we have had him since he was eight weeks old, but he is sad because he is alone too much. I will be sad for awhile but I must do what is best for this sweet dog.

As I open the door to my apartment and am thinking it feels good to be home I hear a dripping in the bathroom. I set my food down and go to investigate. I see the bathtub has started to overflow. Oh no. I guess somehow the plug for the tub is covering the drain and the water is turned on at a trickle. Geez this cannot be real. I am searching the cupboard for towels to mop up water.

Lovely, all the towels are dirty and of course they must be in my sons room.

I wade through his messy room looking for towels. I find six towels, mop up the water and empty the tub. I take all the wet towels outside to hang on the railing to dry. I am in no mood to deal with yet another incident. I call my son at work to see if he has any knowledge of this incident. Surprise! Surprise! He has no idea. He tells me he has to hang up because he is busy at work. I am in such a bad mood I cannot resist saying "oh I thought you were at the beach," then he says "huh, what are you talking about?" I simply hang up. I realize I am in dire need for a mental health day myself. I decide that after I eat I am calling Liz to discuss our next trip to the beach.

So I dial up Liz and she can hardly believe what I am telling her about my day. First she asks me how many glasses of wine I have had? Finally she believes I am stone cold sober. We agree that we should plan a mental health day soon. Looks like we are going to do a Wednesday to break up our week. Next week sounds good. We are kind of afraid to do this week with me just getting back and all the problems with Steffy. Sheryl is most likely in a bad mood from dealing with Steffy today. I tell Liz that Steffy could barely walk at the end of the day. Liz says "I can't wait to see what shoes Steffy shows up in tomorrow."

We say goodnight and I watch a little television and call my friend Marilyn to tell her the sordid details of my life.

CHAPTER

1 9

BZZZ, BZZZ, BZZZ. I keep pushing the button but the noise won't stop. I feel like I am not nearly ready to get up. I drag myself to the dresser and closet grabbing clothes and head to the bathroom. I would like to stand under this hot shower all day, and then I remember my electric bill. I am going over things in my mind. Today should be most interesting. I remind myself that I need to find out exactly what Steffy's actual work hours are?

I am heading into the lab parking lot still half asleep. I am going to have to go in the back door to Urgent Care and steal a cup of coffee out of the break room or I will never be able to get through this morning.

Thank goodness the coffee is hot and fresh. I try and pick a coffee cup that does not look like anybody's favorite and now I am heading down the hall with coffee in one hand and backpack over my other shoulder.

As I get to the door of the lab I see two old ladies having

a rather loud discussion and five or six other people in line behind them. Apparently the ladies are in disagreement over whether or not Dr. Sweeney is leaving his wife for one of his nurses. "Excuse me ladies" I say, "I just need to get in here to open the door." Nobody is moving.

"Sorry honey but you are dead wrong" says one of the women. The other one comes back at her with a very loud "where have you been the past five years? You need to put your damn glasses on and pay attention. I just saw them in the break room last time I was here and he was giving his nurse a thorough exam."

"Ladies I need to get in here to open the door." They are shifting to one side now. I get the key in to open the door and now these ladies have forgotten all about Dr. Sweeney and are focused on being first in line at the front counter. "Please sign in and have a seat folks and I will get you all in and out as quickly as possible." One lady is asking me if she can be first because she only has a urine test? I say "of course." This raises some eyebrows but nobody says anything. So I point her to the bathroom and give her instructions as I grab the clip board to call the next patient.

The next patient is Dorothy Scott. "Good morning" I say as she makes her way to the window. "Good morning Dear" she replies. "May I please see your insurance cards?" As she is handing me her Costco card Liz walks in and glances toward us and giggles. Looks like it is going to be another fun day here at the outpatient lab. Liz heads into the break room in the back and closes the door. She is most likely *checking the specimen*.

"Dorothy, do you have your insurance card?" "I just gave it to you" she says. "Ma'am, that is your Costco card." "Oh dear, let me look for that other card" she says. All I can do is wait. Finally she says "here it is, can you just get it out for me?" As she tries to hand her wallet over to me her hand slips, the wallet falls open on the counter and all of her stuff is falling all over the counter and the floor. As I am down on my hands and knees picking up the contents of her wallet off the floor Liz walks out of the break room and smiles and says "are we having fun yet? And when you get a chance can you go back and *check the specimen*?" I guess it is my turn at the Scrabble game.

I sift through the cards, pick out the ones I need and hand Mrs. Scott her wallet back. "Please have a seat and someone will call you back soon" I tell her. I register a few more patients.

The phone rings and it is a business sounding man on the other end. He says "yes I am calling to see about making an appointment for you to send somebody out to my office to draw my blood." "Sir could you hold for just a moment?" I call out to Liz and let her know that there is a call for her on line one. Perfect call to get Liz irritated on this beautiful day. Gotcha! I am chuckling to myself as I hear her pick up the phone and in her bright cheerful voice say "this is Liz, may I help you." She is now leaning around the corner, looking at me and rolling her eyes.

Stunts like this is what helps us make the time fly and get through each day. "No sir we do not do that" I hear her say. "I am sure you are a very important man," I hear her say. I am giggling to myself as I call the next patient up to the front window. Then I hear Liz say "sir could you hold for just a moment?" She walks out of the room and immediately calls a patient back to draw their blood. Oh my, this is new. Liz must really be fed up, I wonder how long this guy will sit on hold before he hangs up?

I decided I better pick up the line and try and appease this man so we don't get a call from Sheryl. "Sir, thank you for waiting. Do you need the address to our office?" I ask. "Yes I do" he says. I give him the address and he says "what the hell is going on over there? I really don't appreciate being put on hold this long." "Sir, we have a lot of patients waiting to have their blood drawn, I need to hang up now." "You know never mind, I am going to find me a better lab with friendlier people" he says as he hangs up. I am so grateful.

Right now I am realizing that Liz and I cannot have our beach mental health day soon enough.

I call the next patient up to the window and I see Steffy come in through the front door. I ask her if she can please come sit in the front and register people as I see Liz come out and call another patient back. Then I notice that something is not quite right about the way Steffy looks today. Oh no she is wearing purple slippers and purple scrubs. I seriously do not have the patience for this right now.

I lean my head in Liz's doorway and announce that I will be *checking on the specimen* for the next hour if she needs me. She laughs. That wretched bitch just did a forty eight point word on our Scrabble board. Damn her. Okay, time for me to make one of my letters a blank. I just turn it backwards to the blank side.

I hear Liz through the door asking Steffy where her damn shoes are? She is trying to explain to Liz why she is wearing slippers. You can't make this stuff up. Steffy is telling Liz that her feet are too sore and tired from yesterday and she does not want to be uncomfortable all day. I think our newest employee is a little cream puff and just may need some special care.

Liz is looking bored to tears as Steffy goes on with her story. I wonder what Liz will say to her? I can hear Liz asking her how her meeting with Sheryl went? I silently close the door and let Liz deal with her. One thing for sure is that Liz and I are both sick of babysitting this twelve year old phlebotomist every day.

Perfect, I just used my Q on a triple letter and then the word is doubled. Liz will be shocked.

Liz walks in the door and slumps into the chair looking disgusted. She says "that girl is not normal." "No kidding" I say. So Liz says she is just going to leave her in her slippers and make her do more draws. "Maybe the patients will complain more about Steffy if we spend more time back here?" Liz says. I remind her that a lot of our patients do not want her drawing their blood.

As we talk more we realize we need a break this Friday. So all we have to do is get through today and tomorrow. "Are you in the mood for Chinese?" I ask her. "Hmmm yes sounds real good" she says. Liz offers to go get it. We hear some commotion out front but neither of us moves. I open our stash drawer where we keep the menus' for various food places nearby plus a supply of soy sauce, fortune cookies, plastic forks and salt and pepper packets. We are selecting what we want from the supposedly fast Chinese place that in reality is slower than a snail's pace. I lean my head out the door asking Steffy if she wants anything from the Chinese place? She says no and tells me her boyfriend is taking her out to lunch to a nice place. I try not to laugh as I close the door.

I relay the message to Liz. We both laugh at the same time. So her boyfriend is taking her out to lunch with slippers on? He must be just like her? I ask Steffy what time she is taking her lunch? "One p.m. if that is okay?" "Okay that is fine" I say. Liz heads out the door and I head out to the front to see what is going on?

Steffy has made herself comfortable up front and there are two patients waiting. Steffy has called one of them up to the window to get them registered.

After she registers one I call them back to draw their blood. As Mrs. Johnson takes a seat she says "I am so glad I got you. That girl with the purple hair and nose ring is not good at drawing blood. Is she right out of school?" "I have no idea, but it certainly seems like it" I reply. I am glad this lady came in today because Friday will be ugly here in the lab. I wish her well and head to the processing room with her blood. As I walk out I hear voices. Steffy's boyfriend has arrived to pick her up.

Oh my. She must be proud. He is wearing a stained up Coors beer t shirt and flip flops. As I look closer he has a matching gold nose ring. What a beautiful couple! I am imagining little miniature people running around who look just like them. Could you just picture little third grade kids arriving at school with nose rings to match mom and dad. Steffy and her boyfriend head out of the lab. I simply cannot resist going to the window to see what kind of car he has? Geez no surprise here, he is on a motorcycle. Alright back to work. I make a note to ask Steffy what her hunk of a man does for a living?

I see Mrs. Stevens sitting in the waiting room. I wish Liz was here because this lady is exactly the type of patient I would hand off to Liz. I call Mrs. Stevens up to the window and get her order and tell her I will be with her shortly. The phone rings and it is Urgent Care saying they have a draw for us. I tell them I am alone right now and will be down shortly. I call Mrs. Stevens back to draw her blood. "Good afternoon" I say. "Oh is it afternoon dear?" she asks. As I start getting my stuff out to draw her blood I say "excuse me." Liz has just walked in with our Chinese food. I ask if she can go do the draw down in Urgent Care? Okay we should both be able to eat together when Steffy comes back.

The minute I walk back into the draw room Mrs. Stevens asks me what tests have been ordered? I tell her the names of the tests. Next she asks if there is a test for her memory? I say no. She asks if there is a test for stomach pains and diarrhea? I tell her no. "Well why are we doing blood tests if they are not for my current problems?" "Ma'am I don't know why your doctor ordered these tests you need to talk to him about that." Now she wants to know if I can call him and ask? "No, I believe he is at lunch right now" I tell her. "Well I am getting really mad" she says. "Do you still want your blood drawn today?" I ask. "No. I am driving over to my doctors office right now." Okay fine. I wish her the best and send her on her way.

As I head to the processing room Liz walks in with the blood from Urgent Care. I call the courier to come get the STAT. Liz starts getting our lunch ready. Steffy walks in and I ask her to cover the front while we eat. Wow it is nice having a chance to talk to Liz. I tell her that Steffy's boyfriend is just like her. "Well that figures" she says. "So tomorrow are we going to the beach?" I ask. "Yep let's do it" she says. I guess we are to the point where we just cannot wait until next week. We discuss the details and enjoy our lunch. We agree to meet at ten a.m. and go have fish and chips and then head out to relax on the sand. I ask her what time she is calling in sick?

She says she calls at five a.m. when she gets up. I think I will call at six.

I walk up to the front to see what is going on while Liz makes her way to the front counter with her stuff. She is ready to leave for the day and stops to see what is going on? I am asking Steffy why she has one slipper and one bare foot? She explains to me that one of the slippers fell off as they were going fifty miles an hour. "So what are you planning to do?" I ask her. She looks at me like she has no idea what I am talking about? Liz snickers and says "you ladies have fun now and then adds "see ya wouldn't want to be ya" as she heads out the door laughing. I have no idea what in the hell to do now. Urgent Care calls with a draw so I just send her down the hall barefoot.

Two minutes later Mary from Urgent Care calls and says "we have a problem." She proceeds to tell me that they have a phlebotomist down there who is barefoot. I just say "oh really?" She informs me that they cannot have this going on. I say okay I will be down shortly. As Steffy walks into the office I ask her if she has any shoes in her car? She says no. I ask her to please call Sheryl and explain the problem to her. I have to walk away in order to not laugh as she is explaining her dumb ass story to Sheryl. I can hear Sheryl through the phone yelling "what?" Wonderful, Sheryl is sending her home and docking her pay. Now I have to do all the work for the next three hours.

That is it for me. No guilt whatsoever for taking a mental health day tomorrow. I head down to the Urgent Care with my kit. The patient is a young woman about eighteen years old and they want a pregnancy test. I agree to run the test right in the office for them and should be able to report the results in twenty minutes or so. As I get back to the office there are three patients waiting.

I explain to them that I will not be able to draw anymore blood for the next thirty minutes because I have to run a test in the back. What else can I do? People are looking at me as if they are not sure if they heard me wrong? One man asks "is this a joke?" "No it isn't, the draws for Urgent Care are a priority over other draws and I am only one person here in the lab right now." "I am calling the main lab and filing a complaint" he says. I give everyone Sheryl's phone number and then head to the back to run the test. Amazing what corporate people will do to save a buck.

So I finish the Pregnancy test and head down the hall to deliver the result. When I return to the office it is empty. I bet Sheryl's phone is ringing off the hook. I guess I will get some results ready to go down to the other end of the hall to Primary Care and when I get back I will call Dotty. I am always relieved when nobody is at the counter and I can just drop off the results at Primary Care. This way I do not get stuck answering stupid questions. I am going to attempt to call Dotty. Dotty answers the phone and I ask if she can chat?

She says yes. I ask how she likes it there? First thing she says is "what is up with all the donuts?" I have gained ten pounds since I got here. I ask her if any more patients have been fighting at the back door? I tell her the story about those two old guys with the donuts. She says it is okay working here but Doug hardly does any work. I just laugh. I tell her I hope she gets out of there soon. I tell her that Steffy is out of control and that I have a feeling that she will get a call about six thirty tomorrow morning saying she needs to go to Whitney Park. I am so hoping the last hour of the day will be quiet.

Boy I almost wish I could be alone after Liz leaves just like the old days. This is peaceful. The phone rings and it is Liz. I tell her about Urgent Care making me go down and do the draw because Steffy went down there barefoot. Liz just sighs. Liz says she is starting to make dinner now so we hang up.

I head to the back to make sure all the processing is caught up. Looks good back here. Almost quitting time. I start thinking about which weird tests Liz and I can call into the office tomorrow while we are sitting on the beach. There are so few tests that Dotty and Steffy actually know it should not be difficult to come up with a few.

As I am driving home it occurs to me that I can call in sick tonight at bedtime and sleep in a little tomorrow morning. I am going to drive through Taco Bell tonight so I do not have to deal with cooking anything for dinner. Time to turn on the tv and relax. I hope we don't get in trouble for both being gone on a Friday? We figure it is worth the risk because we are both getting so burned out.

Boy there's something wonderful about relaxing and watching tv knowing that you can sleep in a little bit longer the next morning. I think I shall make some popcorn.

CHAPTER

2 0

WOW I WAKE UP IN A PANIC thinking I overslept, then I remember that today is my mental health day. I take a leisurely shower and enjoy a cup of coffee and a piece of toast. This sure is nice not being rushed. Liz is coming by to pick me up and we will head out to the coast. I am thinking about the delicious fish and chips, can't wait to head out to the coast. I start gathering my beach chair, beach bag and snacks and I hear a horn honking so Liz is here. Yippee, here we go. Liz is irritated with her husband but she will snap out of it quickly when we reach the coast. I notice her driving gets a bit faster than normal at the mention of his name.

We sit out on the patio enjoying our fish and chips and visit. The sun feels so good, this is wonderful. The lady that owns this place makes her tartar sauce fresh from scratch. It is incredible. Now we are heading out to the beach, it sure does feel good to be out at the coast. The lab is really getting on my very last nerve these days.

Wow! This is a beautiful day at the beach. As we settle into our chairs and breathe in the fresh sea air I can feel myself relax. Liz looks pretty happy too. We just sit in silence for a good fifteen minutes. Honestly, this really is a mental health day and I think it should be required twice a month. I am always in a better mood after a day at the beach.

Liz says "wanna go for a walk?" Of course I want to go for a walk. There are very few people out on the beach today and it looks like low tide will happen in about three hours. We could not have timed this any better.

After walking about a mile we turn around and head back to our spot on the beach. We decide that after we enjoy a beer we will call the lovely ladies at the lab and ask them about lab tests that they should be familiar with but actually know nothing about. We were feeling a bit guilty about bothering them but decided that it is so much fun we couldn't resist.

The sun feels so good. We are both just daydreaming as we soak up the sun and watch a couple of dolphins playing. I would love to just live out here in my tent.

Liz and I are discussing who might be running the lab.

I am thinking Steffy and Dotty, but who really knows. Liz is mulling over in her head any tests that I may have missed that they definitely will not know. I am thinking a fun one will be the semen analysis. This will drive them crazy with embarrassment and there are very specific instructions they must tell the patient, this will be a lot of fun.

It looks like Liz has just received a call from Sheryl. I am trying to catch what is being said but all I hear is Liz saying "uh huh, uh huh, okay goodbye." Liz says that Sheryl was asking her questions about our favorite twelve year old phlebotomist Steffy. Apparently Sheryl has already received two complaints and it is only noon.

Sheryl wanted to find out if Liz has had problems with Steffy? It looks like Steffy was telling Sheryl that Betty has been picking on her and making her feel afraid. Sheryl wanted to know if Steffy has told Liz that she is feeling afraid because there are too many rules in Whitney Park.

Liz said yes, Steffy did tell me that. Then Liz told Sheryl that Steffy has no idea how to dress as a professional and that she has had to send her home repeatedly for wearing inappropriate shoes. This is not rocket science here. Steffy sees how we all dress. It is as easy as monkey see monkey do here. Even Steffy should be able to figure this out.

Liz hangs up the phone and starts laughing hysterically. Liz says "can you believe it? Steffy told Sheryl the night she went there after work that we are both being mean to her and that she is feeling afraid?" Liz is telling me that Sheryl sounds very irritated and is probably going to have to fire her. According to Liz the wearing slippers to work and going down to Urgent Care barefoot was the last straw. "But what will we do for laughs without Steffy there?" I say to Liz.

"Speaking of Steffy, shall we call the lab and see which clowns are working? I suggest we ask them for instructions for our pseudo husband on how to collect the sample for a semen analysis. "Oh I forgot about that test" Liz says as she is laughing.

We get ourselves all settled in and comfortable, turn the volume up on the phone and set it on the ice chest between us. Liz is saying she remembers all the specifics about the collection. There are certain requirements that must be met. The patient has to follow the instructions to the letter. He must have had no ejaculation for at least two days and the specimen must be collected by masturbation with no lubricant. Specimen must be kept at body temperature and is only collected at the main lab so they can run the test within the hour. Well this should be a scream! Liz is dialing the phone and covering her mouth with a Kleenex to disguise her voice.

"SuperLab, may I help you?" Steffy says. Oh perfect! I have to turn my back to Liz so we don't start laughing. Liz starts in with her story about needing instructions for her husband to collect a semen analysis? "What is that?" Steffy asks. Liz says in her sweetest fake voice "you are the professional that is why I called the lab. This is the lab right?" "Ugh, yes it is" Steffy says. Silence. "Can you please hold while I look the test up and get the information for you?" "Okay" Liz says. We finish drinking our beers in silence as we wait for our brilliant co-worker to return to the phone with the information.

Steffy says "it is going to take me a few more minutes and I will be right back, okay?" Liz says "okay I will wait." Geez we could plant a garden it is taking so long. "How much do you want to bet she had to call Sheryl?" I say. "Hello?" Steffy says. Liz swallows her mouth full of beer and says, yes I am here. "Okay well" Steffy begins "he has to collect his semen in a cup at the lab." "Oh I see" says Liz. "How exactly does he do that?" Liz asks. At this point I am doubled over laughing. I almost choke as Liz asks Steffy if there are any rules or specific instructions about what he needs to do? "Ummmm can you hold for a minute?" she says. "Oh sure" Liz says. This is hysterical. Liz puts the phone on mute as we are bent over laughing. I know this is a pathetic game but it sure does make us laugh.

Steffy is back on the line and Liz unmutes the phone. "Ma'am" she says "there's a bunch of instructions can you come by and pick them up?" "No I am sorry but I need you to just give me the instructions now over the phone. Is that a problem? May I speak to your supervisor please?" "No, there is no supervisor here. Can you hold please?" We can hear the phones ringing and lots of commotion in the background. After about ten minutes Steffy comes back on the line.

"Okay ma'am are you there?" "Yes, I am still here" Liz says. Steffy tells Liz that she has some information for her. "Great, can you give it to me slow because I am taking notes" Liz says as she takes another swig of her beer.

"I will read the instructions to you. The specimen must be collected by ummm, I can't pronounce it, so I will spell it" Steffy tells Liz. Liz mutes the phone again as I cannot stand it anymore and spit my beer out while laughing out loud. So Steffy is spelling *masturbation* for Liz. I thought I would just die when Liz says "I don't know if my husband knows how to do that?" At this point I am laughing out loud. Steffy asks Liz what she means and Liz proceeds to ask if there are specific instructions for her husband on how to do this masturbation technique? Now I literally fall out of my chair and onto the sand laughing.

Liz says "okay go ahead and give me the special instructions." "Well there is another word that I don't know what it is so I will spell it for you." Steffy spells *abstain* for Liz. Liz says oh okay, pronounces the word for Steffy in her fake sweet old lady voice and tells Steffy what the word means. As Steffy continues to do her best to try to explain the procedure Liz is yawning. I think she is rapidly losing interest in this game.

"Ma'am I am all alone in the lab right now and I have a whole waiting room stacked up with people. Can you call the main lab?" Liz replies with a definite no and tells Steffy that she needs to finish giving her the instructions. Steffy finally finishes reading the instructions to Liz and we hear a loud noise in the background.

As Liz hangs up the phone we both laugh some more. Liz says "sounds like the lab is a mess over there." I am picturing phones ringing, patients waiting and protesting loudly and who knows what else. Just thinking about the mess makes me laugh. I think I have been doing this job, way too long.

Wow! I am thinking of Steffy all alone at the lab with a waiting room full of angry patients when I get an additional visual of Sheryl's phone ringing off the hook with complaints. This is very entertaining for Liz and I. We decide to take a short nap and then we will call again to educate the little darling a bit more. I am starting to wonder how Steffy ever passed all the tests to become a phlebotomist?

We wake up an hour later and now it's my turn to call the lab and educate our twelve year old fellow phlebotomist. I have selected another test I am ninety nine percent positive she has never heard of. My phone is on speaker so we can both enjoy the entertainment. I have my fake voice established and feel ready. The phone is ringing and ringing until the answering machine comes on. I decide to leave a nasty message about what kind of business is this where nobody answers the phone. I leave a fake phone number just to give her something more to handle. Liz is bent over spitting out her beer laughing.

Thirty minutes later I am dialing again. After the fourth ring Steffy answers and sounds out of breath. She asks me to hold. Great. Liz hands me another ice cold beer. Five minutes later Steffy is asking if she can help me? I try not to laugh. So in my best fake voice I ask her what I need to do to collect stools for a helicobacter pylori test? "Ummmm, what is it called?" I can hear her scrambling for a pen to write with. I patiently spell it out. "Okay, can you please hold while I look it up?" "Sure no problem" I say. "Ma'am I am back with you are you there?"

"Yes, I am here." "From what I can see here you need to collect some stool in some bottles called a para pak." "Okay, how much stool? And do you have the para pak there for me to pick it up?" "Ummm can you hold while I check?" I say yes. Liz and I are just chatting while we wait for her to check on this very common test that she should already know about. Fifteen minutes later Steffy comes back on the line and tells me that yes they have the para pak bottles and that she to go now. I am getting a bit irritated and let her know that she may not hang up until she finishes giving me the answers to the questions I have about this test. "Now I need to know how much stool I need to collect and do I keep it at room temperature or does it need to be refrigerated?"

I stretch out in my chair and figure that I can close my eyes while I wait. Liz and I are talking about how things have changed with this new generation of workers. We are trying to figure out what happened?

"I am back with you" Steffy says as she returns to the phone. "It looks like the specimen needs to be refrigerated and transported to the lab within twenty four hours of collection. "Oh okay, so I can collect it Friday night and bring it in on Monday?" I ask. "Sure that should be fine" she says. Apparently Steffy has no concept of time. I say to myself "seriously?" Liz is just shaking her head in disbelief and motioning for me to hang up.

So I thank Steffy for the instructions and hang up. Liz and I are talking and wonder how many patients may have been given the wrong instructions by Steffy? We agree to take a break and call back one more time at four thirty or so as a fun way for whoever we get on the phone to wrap up their day.

Boy that nap was so nice. Liz and I are enjoying watching some boats going by, time sure flies out here.

It seems like Steffy has been alone in the lab all day because as we make our last phone call to the lab she answers. It is Liz's turn to call and of course Steffy has never heard of the protein total quantitive urine test that she is calling about. This is a test where the patient has to collect all of their urine over a twenty four hour period in containers provided by the lab.

Again, this is a basic test that Steffy should be familiar with. We are not surprised to be getting the same results as we did during the previous prank calls to the lab. After Liz goes back and forth with questions Steffy can not answer she finally ends the call while rolling her eyes. We both hear yelling in the background as she hangs up. A patient must be angry.

We both look at each other as we realize just how little our coworker actually knows. Perhaps being a massage therapist would be a better career for her.

Liz and I kick back for awhile longer while contemplating making a bet on how many complaints will be waiting for us on Monday. I shudder to think about what kind of messes will be waiting for me when I unlock the door Monday morning.

Liz and I decide to pack it in about six thirty p.m. This way we can miss the traffic. As we are driving back to civilization my phone rings. Crap, it is Sheryl. I answer in my fake sick sounding voice. "Betty, do you think you will be coming into work on Monday?" I clear my throat and cough and say I am just driving back from the doctor's office and he says I do not have strep throat, so yes I will be there.

Sheryl says that she is going to have to hire another float phlebotomist in case Steffy is not there or for times when myself or Liz are out sick. "Is everything alright?" I ask. "Not exactly" says Sheryl.

Apparently there were lots of problems today. Dotty had a family emergency and was unable to come in and Steffy was alone. "Oh no" I say. "Steffy was there until almost six p.m. and I am not sure everything was processed? Please call me on Monday and let me know what you find when you arrive." "Will do" I say as we hang up. Liz just sighs and says she wishes she could quit. I honestly am afraid to arrive on Monday and see what the office looks like.

CHAPTER

2 1

AS I WALK DOWN THE HALL MONDAY morning I can feel something is not right. First of all there is nobody in line. As I reach the door I notice the lights are on. I try the handle and it is open. Uh oh. I walk in and there are seven people sitting there staring at me. I say good morning to everyone as I walk through the door to the back. I put my stuff in the break room and start checking on things.

I discover all the machines in the front room are still running. As I approach the processing room I see several requisitions in bags but no tubes of blood to go with them. As I head to the front counter I notice there are papers everywhere and the printer is gone. Apparently there were no results delivered. Both of the phone lines are ringing and all I can do is let them go to voice mail.

I grab my lab coat and call the first patient. I am afraid this is going to be the longest day ever. As I start to register this patient I realize we have a major problem. The computer is gone. Oh my. As soon as Liz gets here I will need to call Sheryl with more good news.

In the meantime I will have to go back to doing things the old way and just attach copies of the patients insurance cards to the requisition. Oh no the copy machine is gone also. Maybe I will get a day off?

I guess I can hand write the insurance information on each requisition. This will mean we have an endless line all day. Liz is going to be in a very bad mood when she gets here. There are now twelve people in line. I call Sheryl and leave a message informing her of our situation.

I call the first patient. I feel bad because I know she has been waiting for a long time. I hand write all of her information on the requisition. Man this is awful. As Mrs. Jones takes a seat in the blood draw chair she proceeds to tell me that she was at the office on Friday and it was an absolute mess so she walked out. I ask her what was going on? She says the strange girl who looks like she belongs in the circus was all alone. There was an hour wait. She proceeds to tell me that Steffy was an hour late opening the office and that she seemed like she was high on something. All I said was oh my. As I am heading to the processing room Liz walks in.

"What the hell is going on?" she says. I ask her if she can please carry on while I call Sheryl? I am trying to dial Sheryl and Liz is loudly commenting about where the hell is the computer? I tell her that she needs to write everything by hand like we did in the old days. She gives me a you have got to be kidding look as she takes a seat at the front desk. Liz asks if Dotty is coming in? I say I believe so.

Sheryl comes on the line and says "Betty what the hell is going on down there? I have already had three complaints. I begin explaining the whole sordid story to Sheryl.

Sheryl tells me to call the police from the back room so they can take a report. She says that if Steffy shows up I am to send her straight to the main lab to see her. Uh oh, I bet Sheryl cans her. I ask Liz to register a few people while I make that call and then I can start drawing blood with her.

The police will be coming by in a couple hours during lunch and we are going to have to close the office for an hour. Sheryl was livid when I told her the lab was left unlocked and stuff scattered everywhere. She nearly had a stroke when I told her computer, monitor and printer were all stolen. I would love to be a fly on the wall when Steffy meets with Sheryl. Apparently I will be paid an extra hour for not getting a real lunch hour. Ten a.m. and in wanders Steffy.

Before I tell her to go to Sheryls' I need to ask her why the paperwork is on the counter and where is the blood to go with it? Steffy tells me she sent the blood with the courier without the paperwork. I cannot believe what I am hearing. Next she proceeds to explain why the office was left unlocked and why the place is a mess. I ask her if the tubes of blood were labeled and she says she cannot remember. I just give her a disgusted look and tell her that Sheryl wants to see her immediately.

I bring the paperwork to the front and wait to hear from Sheryl. Meanwhile both phone lines are ringing with doctors offices looking for results. I have to ask Sheryl if there are tubes of blood up there with no paperwork. If not I have to call the patients in to be redrawn. I think they should make Steffy call the patients and then fire her ass.

I am beginning to get a headache. I am pretty sure this is the last we will see of Steffy. She was telling me that things were going very well until she had two patients in a row that she could not get the blood drawn and then she got upset and her boyfriend came over to comfort her. Then things got a little crazy and she just had to leave. She said she did try to call Sheryl and she was not there.

Holy cow I guess she just literally got in her car and left. I cannot wait to see who we get next as a phlebotomist to help us out.

Liz offers to go get us some lunch if I will switch places with her and take a seat at the front counter. We only have four people left in the waiting room. This day is getting to be a drag. The phone rings and it is Sheryl. I give her the good news about having paperwork here on two patients and no blood. She says she will go back to the processing area and play hunt for the blood.

Steffy should be arriving at the main lab anytime. I ask Sheryl if we will be having a new phlebotomist down in Whitney Park next week? She says "yup." Well Liz will be thrilled to not have to deal with Steffy anymore, but who will we get next?

Liz walks in the door with lots of Chinese food. Oh boy I am starving. The good news is they did not steal our Scrabble game. It is my turn. Liz and I are pretty evenly matched. Well we get three quarters through our lunch when somebody is ringing the bell. So we do rock/paper/scissors to see which one of us has to head up front to the window. Liz lost so out she goes. Oh no, I hear Mrs. Brown asking for me at the window. She is telling Liz that she must speak to me immediately.

Liz comes to get me and she has a big grin on her face. She says your friend is here to see you. I thank her and head out while getting my lab coat on. I call Mrs. Brown back to my blood draw chair. As she sits down she is giddy with excitement. As soon as I reach for her arm she says hold on. I wait patiently as she pulls something out of her purse. She is pulling out a pink revolver. "Oh my!" I say. "Look what I bought" she says. "It's not loaded is it" I ask. "No, but I have bullets in the bottom of my purse. I was hoping you could show me how to load it."

"Wow, where did you find that?" I ask her. "I bought it at a gun store over by the Taco Bell. It was easier to buy my house than it was to buy this gun. I had to wait to get it though. I cannot believe how hard it was to get this really cute gun" she continues. "The man at the gun store was very nice. He said this is the perfect gun for my small hands and he pointed out that it matches my shirt."

I am really getting concerned at this point.

"The man at the gun store was very helpful. I told him it was to protect myself. He didn't ask me any more questions about that. I guess in a way I am protecting myself, right?" she says. "Well I don't know?" I tell her. "So I need to practice my position ya know?" she tells me as she is holding the gun up and pointing it around the room.

"Mrs. Brown, what happened to you moving into your daughters house?" "Well she said she doesn't mind me being there, but why should I have to leave my home? Last week Marty and Fred had a poker game and invited all of their nasty, lazy, friends to my house."

"I came home to a huge mess. They ate peanuts and drank beer and the peanut shells are all ground into the floor. I am out of patience with him. So tell me young lady, do I just keep pulling the trigger until this baby is empty?"

"Ma'am I am thinking you should rethink this whole

idea," I tell her. "Do you want to help me?" she asks. "No I do not want to know any more details" I say. "Well after I shoot his privates off I wonder where I should hit him next?" "Mrs. Brown, I think you need to take some time and really think about this plan of yours." Silence, as she is thinking. I tell her that I don't want her to end up in jail as she is aiming at the wall. "Mrs. Brown, have you ever shot a gun before?" "Why no Dear, but how hard can it be?" At this point I am deeply concerned and do not want to hear any more details. "Mrs. Brown have you shown your daughter the gun?" "No dear, but I will show her tonight." "Okay, let us get your blood drawn, so you can be on your way." I tell her. She tucks her new gun into her purse and puts out her arm.

As I finish drawing her blood I ask her if she will promise to go to her daughters for a few days and talk this plan over with her? "Well okay if you think I should." "Yes I think it would be wise" I say. "Mrs. Brown, there must be a better way to get even with him without killing him?"

"Well, I must get busy and call my next patient. Please be careful and let me know how you are doing?" I say. "Okay I sure will" she says, as she walks out clutching her purse tight.

As I come out of my blood draw room Liz says when you get a chance can you *check the specimen*? It looks like we are caught up for the moment so I head to the back to take my turn at our ongoing Scrabble game.

Liz is gathering her things, and getting ready to head for home. "So what was up with your little friend today?" I explained briefly what Mrs. Brown told me and Liz starts laughing. "Wow, what a gutsy old lady" Liz says. I know right? I said. I head up to the front counter, as Liz heads out the door saying, "see ya , wouldn't want to be ya."

Shortly after I get seated and comfortable at the desk Sheryl calls. "Hi Betty, tomorrow I will be sending a different phlebotomist down to your office to fill in for awhile. Her name is Ashley and she is right out of school." Sheryl hears me sigh and says "just for a while until I figure out what is going on with Steffy?" "Oh I assumed you fired her?" I said. "Well that was the plan, but she has now gotten an attorney and is claiming she was having some kind of a mental breakdown because you and Liz were making her work too hard."

"Are you kidding me?" I say. Sheryl says that she wishes she was. Unbelievable! So I ask Sheryl what kind of a worker Ashley is? "I am having a hard time finding a phlebotomist that actually knows how to work. Most of them do not feel the need to rush, ever. Oh and I have to warn you, Ashley wears all black." Sigh. "Sheryl, I need more money if I have to train another twelve year old phlebotomist." Sheryl okay's fifty cents more per hour. I agree and we hang up.

As I sit back down at the desk, I cross my fingers for luck. I really need a few hours of peace and quiet but after about twenty minutes the phone rings. The man on the phone is sounding very strange. He asks me about a stool test and what he needs to do for a stool culture? I tell him to just come pick up containers and I will give him the instructions. He hangs up. I decide to try and read my book. After a bit I head to the bathroom. When I walk out of the bathroom there is a man standing at the window, it is the man who called on the phone.

He asks me to help him with his specimen. I don't understand. He motions for me to come out to the waiting room and there on the floor by his feet is a paper plate with his stools on it. Seriously? What the hell? I close my eyes then reopen them and look again. This is horrifying to me. This is a new low. "What the hell am I supposed to do with this?" I ask him. You would think he would be embarrassed but nope. He says "do whatever you want with it." "Sir, here are the vials and there are instructions, this is a project you do at home. Then you bring only the vials back to the lab. Make sure you put your first and last name, date of birth and collection date on the vials.

I also tell him that he must take the paper plate full of stools outside and dispose of it somewhere. He seems kind of out of it as he picks the plate up and walks to the door. At the same time a woman is walking in the door and holds the door open for him, she gasps as he passes her when she sees what he is carrying. I go into the back room to watch him out the window as he exits the building and throws the plate in the bushes. A woman who was coming up the steps to the Health Center is just standing there with her mouth hanging open. She probably thinks she is seeing things. I go and get the disinfectic spray and spray the waiting room.

I hope this day ends soon. Sadly I know there will be another day just like it tomorrow. Okay only one more hour to go. What could go wrong?

Just as I start to check the mail the phone rings. "Super-Lab, may I help you?" "Uh ya is this the lab?" a man asks. I let him know that yes, he has reached the lab and he tells me that he needs to get his blood drawn and wants to know if he needs to fast?

Well, it depends on which tests your doctor ordered I tell him. Silence on the other end of the phone. "Does your paper say fasting?" I ask him. "I don't see it, but I don't have my glasses on." The other line is ringing so I ask him to please hold. This will give him a chance to gather his thoughts.

I answer the phone and ask them to please hold. I return to the confused patient. "Sir? Thank you for waiting. Were you able to figure out if your requisition says fasting?" I ask him. "No, I will read you the tests." When he gets to glucose and lipid panel I assure him he needs to fast.

So I give him all the information and I start to say good-bye. "Wait" he says. "Are you near the park?" "Sir, I really need to hang up now, I have another patient waiting. The address is on the requisition. I am feeling completely drained.

I head over to turn the lights out in the waiting room to discourage patients from coming in at the last minute. Finally the courier arrives. I head out to lock the front door. This very long day is finally over.

I stop on the way home to buy a few more lottery tickets. As I walk into my apartment it is actually quiet and neat. I hope my son is still alive? Very rarely is it this neat in here. I am so exhausted I just crash onto the couch. I need some extra sleep tonight. I feel like I will explode if I get even one more dumb ass question.

CHAPTER

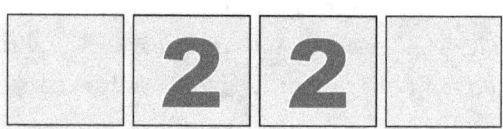

I AM HEARING A BUZZING SOUND and I wish it would stop. I am sort of awake now but start to doze off again. The thought of going into the lab today feels unbearable. I have to pull out of this slump or I will get myself fired. I head for the shower trying not to think about the day ahead and just enjoy the warm water. I slowly start drying myself off and getting dressed when I realize that if I was going any slower I would be going backwards. I see my sons' bedroom door is closed, heaven knows what is going on in there. I am going to have to drive through and get some coffee and breakfast.

I head to work I wonder what our new twelve year old phlebotomist will be like? I drive into the Health Center parking lot and feel tired already. As I walk down the hall towards the lab I can see eight people in line. A few are seated on their walkers and some are leaning against the wall. I give them my usual friendly good morning as I head to the door and unlock it. As we all walk in the door a lady shouts out asking me if

I am the only worker today? I let her know that there will be another phlebotomist here in a half hour. "Well then I guess I should have waited thirty minutes to come in" she says. "Yes that is what I would have done" I tell her. Wow finally a patient who is thinking.

Two more ladies walk in the door and one tells me that they were here the day the girl with the nose ring was going crazy and we left immediately. "Oh I see" is all I can say. I see Liz walking in the door with a stack of magazines for the waiting room. The patients are scrambling to grab a magazine as if she had just dropped hundred dollar bills on the table. The two old ladies are playing tug of war with a magazine. I am stunned. Things just never change. The tug of war ends when I happen to call one of their names.

"Good morning Mrs. Smith" I say as she is digging for her insurance cards. I confirm that she is fasting. Liz is in the break room putting her things away and *checking the specimen*. Meanwhile Mrs. Smith cannot find her insurance cards. "I guess I don't have them" she says. I tell her that it is okay but let her know that she may get a bill. If she does she can just send in a copy of your insurance with the bill.

The phone rings and Liz says she will get it while I keep registering patients. Two minutes later I hear Liz say Bet it's for you. I grab the call as I am trying to register a patient.

Shortly after I take the call I realize it is a difficult patient and Liz gave her to me. Damn her. "Yes ma'am this is the lab" I say. "I am supposed to come in for lab work but I have a few questions and I am heading over there now. Do I just turn left at the light by the huge tree near the school?" "Can you hold please?" I say. I finish registering my patient so she can sit down and I pick up the phone and say "thank you for waiting is there anything else I can do for you?" She continues with more questions. I am going to slap Liz silly. "Well I need to figure out where you are?" I give her the address. She thanks me and tells me that she needs a little more help. I let her know that I have a lot of patients' waiting and that I need to go now.

She continues with more questions "well, I need to know what these tests are for?" "Ma'am can you hold please?"

I call my next patient and ask her what her date of birth is. "Why do you need that?" she says. "So we do not get you mixed up with somebody else" I tell her. She tells me that she doesn't want everyone in the waiting room to know her date of birth so she writes it on a piece of paper, folds it up and slides it over to me. I put a sticky note on top of the requisition with Liz's name on it. Perfect Liz patient. There, gotcha back I say to myself.

As I look up and am just about to call another name in walks our newest phlebotomist. As she heads to the back she says "hello, I was sent here by Sheryl." I say "hi, are you Ashley?" "Just call me A."

"Okay welcome A, you can put your things in the break room and there is a stack of requisitions waiting." I direct her to the empty room where she can draw patients blood. "Fine" she says as she heads back to the room. I am in shock. She looks like somebody from the show *The Walking Dead*. I honestly don't know how much more I can take? I do not think the elderly people are going to want her drawing their blood.

Liz walks out and practically runs into her. Liz puts her hand out and says "I am Liz, who might you be?" She says call me A and keeps walking to the back. Liz says "alrighty then." Liz rolls her eyes as she heads to the pile of requisitions to call the next patient. Oops she has just picked the special patient that I gave her. This will put her in a really foul mood. I continue registering patients. After ten minutes A still has not come out of the back room to draw any blood? I go to check on her and she is sitting in the blood draw chair texting on her phone.

I feel like I am going to explode. I am outside the room counting to one hundred to calm down. Liz walks out of her blood draw room with the blood and looks at me and asks what I am counting? I motion for her to look inside the other blood draw room and I tell Liz that I will buy her lunch if she goes in and explains to our new phlebotomist how things work around here. Liz agrees and I head back up front to register the last few patients.

I am not calling anybody right away because I want to hear what is said between Liz and A in the other room. Liz says "So do you like money?" Silence. Then I hear A say "ya." Liz tells her that nobody sits down in this office until all of the work is done and if I ever see this happen again you will have no job and no money. Simply put. A couple of minutes later the girl walks out in a lab coat and calls her first patient.

The phone rings and it is Sheryl. She is asking how our newest phlebotomist is doing? I tell her that it is too early to tell but that I am not impressed. "Okay, let's give it some time" she says. I say goodbye and am wondering where all of the normal young people are? Liz walks out and I motion for her to follow me to the processing room. I ask her if that is like black eyeliner or what is all around her eyes? She has black scrubs on, black nails and black hair. I honestly do not see how the patients are going to be able to stand to look her in the face and not be scared. All we can do is wait, watch and listen.

As I head back up to the front desk I hear a lady asking A about her makeup? A male patient asks me where the girl from the circus is? I just say "she is out right now."

It is my turn to *check the specimen.* Since we are caught up on work I am going to stay back here as long as possible. I am looking at the Scrabble board. I need forty points to pull ahead. I did the best I could but only made thirty points. As I head out to the front desk I see Liz is in the back room re-drawing A's last patient. This is a routine occurrence with new phlebotomists since they seldom get the blood on the first try.

As I sit down to relax at the front desk I take a deep breath and hear a kaboom. I think something has hit the front door? I open the door to find an elderly woman lying on the ground and her scooter has put a big dent in the front door. "Ma'am are you alright?" I ask, as I offer her my hand to help her up off the ground. "Oh dear, I thought the door was open" she says as she tries to stand up. "No honey the door was closed" I assure her. "I was bringing you my urine sample" she tells me. I am looking around the scooter and on the ground when I see it upside down, partly under the front of the scooter. I head to the back to get some gloves.

Geez she has put her urine in a margarine container and half of it has leaked out onto the carpet in the hallway. I feel ready to scream but nothing is coming out of my mouth. I go and get her two urine containers that I have labeled with her name. Next I get her back on the scooter, give her instructions and get the scooter pointed in the right direction. I hold the doors open for her at the end of the hall and wish her good luck. Out she goes. I head back into the office and I think the big dent in the door is the least of our worries at this point.

"Oh look, it's lunch time." I go back and ask Liz what she wants from the Chinese place. I head out to get lunch. I guess the new girl will go to lunch whenever. As I head out in the car I have a fantasy of just driving off into the sunset and keep going until I run out of gas and then settle there. Maybe I am losing my freaking mind. As I arrive at the Chinese place I notice the line is out the door. I think I will just close my eyes in the car for a few minutes until the line goes down.

Thirty minutes later I wake up. Surprise, there is no line. So I get our food and head back to the lab. I can only imagine what is going on at the lab? When I walk into the lab with the food it is deathly quiet. There are no patients at the moment. This makes me want to jump up and down with excitement. I open the door to the break room and Liz is sitting there *checking the specimen*. A is in the back room talking on her phone. As I set the food down I say "how goes it?" Liz says, "our new employee is a freak. And a lazy one at that." "Tell me how you really feel" I say as I chuckle out loud.

Liz says A did six draws in an hour and I had to redraw half of them. Seriously? I say. Yep and I think she spooks the patients' with that black crazy stuff around her eyes. The phone rings and it is Urgent Care. They have a draw. We do rock/paper/scissors to decide which one of us has to go tell her there is a draw in Urgent Care and we would like her to go do it. I lose. As I walk into the back room A does not look up. I inform her that we need her to go do the draw. She asks what she is supposed to do down there?

I tell her that she needs to go draw a patient at Urgent Care now and that I will be here if she has any problems. Thirty minutes later Bill from Urgent Care is on the phone saying I need to come down there. I grab a kit and two pairs of gloves and head down to Urgent Care. Bill says "she is in room two." As I move the curtain aside and walk into the area where the patient is asleep on a gurney, A is sitting on a stool on her phone. I clear my throat to get her attention. She looks up and says "I tried my best." I want to slap her silly. "The old lady won't let me touch her anymore." I check the patients hospital bracelet and start getting out supplies to draw her blood.

At this point I do not even want to speak to our new phlebotomist. Our elderly lady opens her eyes briefly, sees me and says "thank God you are here." I proceed to draw her blood, gather my things and head back to the lab. I am fairly certain A is still sitting on the stool in Urgent Care playing with her phone. Liz looks at me as I walk into the back office with the blood and without our new phlebotomist. Liz says "did you lose our new friend? I just grunt. Liz tells me that she has called for the courier and they should be here anytime. Meanwhile Liz says it is my turn to *check the specimen* as she gathers her things to go home.

As I am sitting at the front counter Liz says "see ya, wouldn't want to be ya" as she heads out the door.

I dial Sheryl and leave a message for her to please call me. Just as I hang up our courier arrives. I hand Tim the blood and sit back down at the front counter, hoping for a quiet afternoon. Sheryl calls and after I give her the sordid details she tells me to send A back to the main lab if and when I see her. I say "will do" and hang up. I head to the back room to take my turn at Scrabble. Damn that Liz, she just did a fifty point word. I finish my turn and head to the front.

I open my book and read a few pages. As the front door opens I see it is Mrs. Brown. I wish I could magically disappear. "Oh good you are here" she says. I am starting to wish there were several patients waiting, so I would have an excuse to get her to move along. No such luck, I am her captive audience. "Hello there, Mrs. Brown. Are you here for lab work?" "Not today, I want to tell you what happened" she says. "Well last week Fred Watkins managed to catch his garage on fire after his wife had moved him out to the garage to live. So Fred asked my Marty to go down to Mexico on a month long fishing trip while they rebuild the garage. Now I have lots of time to go to the shooting range and practice. I was thinking maybe I should have a company come in and pick the house up and move it while he is gone? How does that sound?" Then she adds "I already called the moving company and I am getting a price quote tomorrow."

"So Mrs. Brown, Marty would come home to a pile of dirt where the house used to be?" "Yes, exactly" she says. "Well I can leave him the garage behind luckily it is not attached. I don't care about the garage anyhow." Personally I am just relieved that she is not still planning to shoot him for now.

"Hey, if I move the house, maybe we can paint the garage pink as a welcome home present? My friends Margie and Louise said they will help me." "Yes, that would be beautiful, let me know how it goes" I tell her. "Okay now I need to hurry up and buy a piece of property to put the house on. I am looking in Arizona right now. Well actually I have a Realtor looking for me and I told them I will give them a huge bonus if they find one fast."

"Oh my, won't Marty be surprised?" I say. "Oh yes he sure will and he has it coming. If you ask me he is getting off easy. Remember I could have shot him. Now at least he gets to live in his pink garage." I must say Mrs. Browns' outlook has seriously improved since she came up with this wild idea. She is giddy with excitement, this is seriously cracking me up! This old lady is very serious about this plan. Two patients walk in so I say goodbye to my little friend for now.

The phone is ringing. Sheryl says "I have good news and I have bad news. The good news is you will be rid of your newest phlebotomist tomorrow." "And the bad news?" "You will be getting Steffy back." As I give a huge sigh Sheryl explains that corporate says we need to keep her for now. "So send the other one back down here and I will find somewhere for her. I briefly filled Sheryl in on how much help she has not been down here. Sheryl laughs and says unfortunately this is our new reality. She tells me to have fun as she hangs up.

I walk to the back room to find A. Yep, there she sits on her ass doing nothing. I tell her that Sheryl wants to see her at the main lab and I walked out.

I see we have two more patients waiting. "Good afternoon" I say as a patient makes her way to the window. She is digging her insurance cards out. "Ma'am these tests are going to require that you fast." "I have not had anything since lunch over two hours ago. I do not have time to drive all the way back here again." I can see her address on the computer and we are talking about a five minute drive at most. "I understand, however your results will not be accurate unless you have been fasting for at least eight to ten hours." "Why does nobody ever tell us this ahead of time?" I suggest that next time she might want to ask her doctor when he gives her the order. "Whatever. You people are impossible to deal with" she says as she walks out the door slamming it behind her.

Oh darn, I so wanted to draw this womans blood and I am devastated at the news that I have one less patient to draw.

I get ready to call the next patient as Steffy walks in. "Hi did you miss me?" she asks. I just look down at the clipboard and say nothing. So today Steffy is wearing purple everything and she appears to be a bit cocky. I guess she feels like she has won and she can get away with anything? She is heading to the back room to put her stuff away.

Steffy walks out towards me in the front office and I notice that she is wearing closed toed shoes. Sheryl has at least taught her about what shoes to wear. Looks like she has on purple tennis shoes.

"Good afternoon ma'am. How are you?" I ask my next patient. "Pretty good. Is there anyone here with a lot of experience?" she asks. "No I'm sorry we are all new." Oh Geez did I really just blurt that out? I get so tired of these questions. Well all I can do now is give her a big smile as she is giving me an uneasy smile. "May I see your insurance cards please?" I ask her. "Mrs. Smith, ummm your insurance cards say Timothy Smith. Did you maybe grab the wrong card?"

"Oh no, I have had these cards a long time. I used to be Timothy but now my name is Margaret. "Oh I see" I say. Are they sending you new cards soon?" "Well dear, they said they were sending me new cards two years ago, so I just keep using these until I get them." I can feel a headache coming on. Why can't I just have an easy day. "Okay, please have a seat and we will call you back shortly." I call Steffy up to do the draw and I go to the back room and dial the insurance company. Yes, apparently this has slipped between the cracks for two years but they are very well aware of the circumstances.

As I head up front the phone rings and it is Jackie at Urgent Care, they need blood drawn for the police STAT. I tell them I will be right down and dial the main lab asking for a courier. I grab the stuff. Apparently the officer is with the suspect in exam room one. This will involve different paperwork and envelopes for chain of custody. I tell Steffy to hold down the fort as I head down to Urgent Care. Thirty minutes later as I walk into the back office I can hear Steffy explaining to a patient that she is a professional and that is why her hair color must match her scrubs and her nails and her shoes.

As I peek in the door the woman has a strange look on her face. She looks confused like she cannot believe what she is hearing come out of this girls mouth. The patient says "well I have never seen a professional dressed like this before?" Steffy proceeds to tell her that this is the new professional look as she turns around in front of the patient like a model would. I am embarrassed for Steffy. The patient is looking at her like she has two heads. Honestly this does not surprise me at all. I head to the processing room to get the blood into the centrifuge.

As I head out of the back room towards the front the woman passes me as she is heading out and whispers to me "I think there is something wrong with that young woman." I just smile and shake my head. Only one more hour to go until this exciting day comes to an end. I hear Steffy yell "that guy who pees on the building is here." I holler back to her "will you please get him registered" as I head to the back room to make sure the machines are on and working properly. I can hear Cedrik's' voice at the front counter.

He is asking for Liz. Steffy tells him that Liz is gone for the day and asks him "what's up with you peeing on the front of our building?" Cedrik says "is purple your natural color?" Steffy responds with "what exactly are you asking me?"

Cedrik says "I'll show you mine if you show me yours."

As I round the corner I see Cedrik has dropped his shorts. This cannot be happening. He is standing at our front counter with his shorts around his ankles and nothing else on. Steffy is smiling.

As I approach the front I ask Steffy "what in the hell is going on?" Steffy calmly explains that Cedrik wants to play a new game of show and tell with her. I tell Cedrik to pull his shorts up and have a seat in the waiting room. I tell Steffy to watch the front while I draw Cedrik's' blood.

Sheryl says we have to just put up with Steffy's' craziness right now and try not to upset her. At first I thought I heard Sheryl wrong but after calling her to clarify what she said I was more irritated than ever before. This is absurd.

I decide to go and bring in the mail and let Steffy open the stool cards. That is her punishment for being unprofessional and stupid. I drop the mail off in front of her without saying a word and then I head to the back room to *check the specimen*. I will take my sweet time until it is quitting time. I wonder if my brilliant coworker will remember to put gloves on when opening the stool cards?

Damn that Liz. She did another fifty point word. I am putting my full concentration into doing a great word. I have to keep up with Liz. After thirty minutes I think forty three points is as good as I can do. I have no idea what is going on in the front office. I am heading out to the front to lock up and go home. Tomorrow will be another exciting day in the loony bin.

CHAPTER

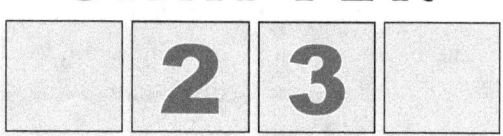

I HEAR A BUZZING. I ignore it and go back to sleep. Oh no I wake up and it is after seven a.m. I guess I will not have time for a shower. This job is getting on my last nerve. I have to figure out a way to make it fun again. I jump into some scrubs and look for my keys. All I have to do is be there physically to open the door. I do not really need to be awake, I could draw the blood in my sleep I have been doing this for so long. Actually I believe I could be naked under my lab coat and nobody would even notice or care as long as I keep drawing the blood and the line keeps moving. I arrive at two minutes before eight.

As I head down the hall I see several of our regular patients. If I take my time registering them I should be able to put a sticky note on some of the requisitions with Liz's name on them. I open the door and everyone races to the clipboard to sign in. A couple of older ladies are fighting to be number one in line. One of them has hit the other one over the head with her purse and is signing in.

I hear a loud voice from the middle of the line. It is Mrs. Nelson. "Ma'am are you all alone? Is this going to take a long time?" I continue registering the patients. When Mrs. Nelson gets to the front of the line she starts peppering me with questions. "I feel really bad" she says. I assure her we will try and get everyone in and out as soon as possible. "Can I lie down?" I take a deep breath and say "why yes of course Mrs. Nelson, let's get you lying down in the back." She is very happy to have all the attention. "Honey I have these pains in my legs and feet, do you think I have a blood clot in my legs?"

"That is a really good question for your doctor" I say as I walk out. Back to registering the next patient. When I get to Mrs. Nelsons' name I put a sticky note with Liz's name on it in the pile. Happy Monday to Liz. When Liz walks in she puts her things away and I tell her "when you get a chance can you please *check the specimen*?" So she heads to the Scrabble game.

As I am registering the last patient the phone rings. "Hello? Is this the lab?" "Yes it is." "Are you open now?" "No sir, I am still at home in bed." There is a pause. "Seriously?" he says. "Sir, I was joking, what can I do for you?" "My doctor gave me a lab slip." "Uh huh" I say. "Can you please tell me what the tests are for?" "Sir, you need to ask your doctor that question. Our job here at the lab is to draw your blood and get the results to your doctor. Alright?" "Okay where are you located?" I recite our address, answer a few more irrelevant questions and end the call. One thing I know for sure is if I am working the window when this man comes in, I will make sure to put a sticky note with Liz's name on it.

Liz tells me that is time for me to *check the specimen*. I can only imagine how far ahead she might be in our ongoing

Scrabble game.

Catch me before I faint. Steffy has just walked in at eight fifty a.m. Ten full minutes early. She says "good morning" as she puts her things away. Today she has purple bracelets on her wrists and a purple scarf around her neck. She stops Liz in the hall and asks her if she looks more professional with the scarf? Liz says "oh ya" and keeps walking. These two can hold down the fort and keep the line moving, it is my turn at Scrabble. As I close the door to the break room where the Scrabble game is I can hear Mrs. Nelson asking Steffy questions. I can't believe it, as I stare at the game I see Liz just did a forty eight point word.

After twenty minutes of sitting at the Scrabble game taking my turn I feel guilty and wrap it up and head out to see how things are going? Liz is going to be blown away. I am only six points behind. The phone rings and it is Jackie at Urgent Care. She says "we have a drug rep lunch today and you guys are all welcome to join us. Today it is Italian food. Wow the day just got better. I thank her as I hang up. "Drug rep lunch" I announced to Liz and her eyes light up. I have to say they really put on quite a spread. Well I guess I will call a patient back and start drawing.

Liz says that Steffy is still on her first patient. "What a genuine surprise" I say. I can see that Mrs. Nelson is next in line. If I go real slow Steffy should get her. I call Mrs. Stevens back. She has been in this lab many times. "Good morning Mrs. Stevens." "Good morning. Boy I am glad I got you" she says to me. "I was afraid I was going to get that girl with the purple hair." I let her know that it is alright for her to ask for one of us if you like." "Oh I didn't know that. Honey, I have been having pains in my hands, do you think I have Arthritis?" "Ma'am I really can't say. I am not a doctor." "Do you see any tests for Arthritis ordered?" "No I don't."

"Why doesn't my doctor ever order the right tests? "Did you ask your doctor to order those tests?" "No, I figured he would know." "Doctors are not mind readers, just tell him what you want. Well there you go, all finished. Your doctor wants a test that requires a urine sample, can you collect that now?" "Yes I think so." "Okay, just leave your specimen in the bathroom and I will take care of it."

As I head to the processing room Liz stops me at the door. She is telling me that she just heard Steffy tell a patient who was dehydrated to go to the lobby and drink a cup of water and then she said well looky there, here is a vein. We all know it does not work that way at all. You need to drink lots of water for several days before you come in for lab work. "Maybe Steffy needs glasses as well as a new brain?" I say. We both laugh. As we walk out Steffy says "I just broke a nail while trying to get Mrs. Nelson up off the bed. I need to go call my girl and see if she can squeeze me in? This just looks so unprofessional." Liz rolls her eyes and heads into the bathroom. I say nothing and head to the front desk as we have been down this road before.

There's a patient at the window.

"Is this the lab?" It is him, I recognize the voice. The latest one who called on the phone asking all sorts of irrelevant questions. Woo hoo! I am giving him to Liz. "Yes this is the Lab." He pulls a crumpled lab slip out of his pocket and hands it to me. It has grease stains and what appears to be catsup all over it. I ask him if he is fasting? "Uh, I believe so." "So is that a yes or no?" I ask. "Ummm I'm gonna say yes."

I ask to see his insurance cards. He pulls out a wallet that looks like it is being held together by a thread. "Here you go" as he drops them on the counter in front of me. "Okay, please have a seat and one of us will call you back soon" I tell him. I immediately pull out a sticky note and put Liz's name on it.

As I head to the processing room Steffy passes me on her way to go get her fake nail fixed. Neither one of us says anything. Unbelievable, I say to myself. It is ten thirty a.m. and we are making bets about how long this will take. Liz heads to the front counter and is calling her special patient back to have his blood drawn. In around two minutes she will be sticking her head around the corner, mouthing something nasty or giving me a not nice hand gesture.

Right on cue she sticks her head around the corner and says "just you wait." I laugh out loud. I am going to work on processing for a few minutes. Spinning the blood down and bagging it so we can get it into the refrigerator until the courier arrives.

I stick my head in the door to where Liz is drawing blood on her special patient. I simply say "I am heading down the hall to see what is out." She sticks her tongue out at me and knows that I am going down to check out the drug rep lunch. Oh boy, this smells incredible. There is salad, lasagna, garlic bread, spaghetti and meatballs. I fill a plate and look through all the samples of note pads, pens and clipboards all printed with various drug logos. I head to a table to scarf down my food. As I am almost finished Liz walks in. She sits down at the table and I ask if Steffy is back? "No" she says. Then we both look at each other and laugh, nobody is in the office. Well this is what happens when management does not appreciate good people.

Five minutes later I head back down the hall. Both phone

lines are ringing, but stop before I can get to the front counter to answer them. There are two patients waiting. I call the next patient up to the window. "Good morning Martha, how are you?" "Fine, thank you." "Martha, you have several fasting tests here. Are you fasting?" "No." "Okay, we need you to come back on a day when you are fasting." "Okay" she says. I tell her that we open at eight a.m. and I go over the fasting requirements. She heads out the door. Why can't more patients be this polite and understanding.

As I get ready to call the next patient Steffy walks in. She has what looks to be a lunch in a separate bag. It is twelve ten p.m. and she apologizes that it took so long. I give no indication that it is a problem for me. She has a lighter shade of purple on all ten fingers. She explains that the girl was out of the other purple color and all ten fingers need to match so she looks professional. I wonder if she ever notices the look on my face as she carries on about being professional. She looks like a hooker in a lab coat. Especially the nose ring.

I call the next patient up to the window. I ask her if she is ready to work now? "Yes, let me get my lab coat" she says.

I call Bill Murphy to the window. "Mr. Murphy, can I please see your insurance cards?" Suddenly I hear the phrase repeated. I feel like I am going nuts, because I don't see anybody else nearby. Mr.. Murphy is standing sideways and as he turns around straight I see a bird on his shoulder. A bird that looks like a parrot. "Mr. Murphy we cannot have your bird in the office." "Oh no my dear this is not just a bird, this is Jack. He is my emotional support pet." "Excuse me?" "Yes, he provides me with emotional support." Now the bird is repeating everything I say and I am thinking to myself you have got to be kidding me. I am suddenly grateful that Steffy is here. I don't have the patience today so this is a perfect Steffy patient.

As Steffy takes Mr. Murphy and his parrot to the back I close my eyes for a few seconds. Liz walks in and I tell her quietly about Mr. Murphy and his parrot. Liz just rolls her eyes. I also let her know it is time for her to *check the specimen.* She looks relieved to be able to head to the back room and relax while she takes her turn at Scrabble. I can hear bits and pieces of the conversation between Steffy and Mr. Murphy. He seems very curious about her all purple everything. The bird is loudly repeating everything they say. Liz walks out and says "I just kicked your ass at Scrabble and started us a new game. Whew Look at the time. Time for me to go home." Great, now I have three hours with Steffy.

As Liz heads out the door I get the usual "see ya wouldn't want to be ya." Today for some reason it makes me chuckle. I see we are low on magazines once again, so I head down to Primary Care to see about stealing some of theirs. I bring back two Time magazines and one Readers Digest. I bet they last four days at the most. As soon as I get around to the front counter the phone rings. I guess I have to answer it because Steffy is still in the back room with her new friend/patient.

"SuperLab may I help you?" I say. "Hi, I need to get some lab tests done. Can you please come to my house?" "No. I'm sorry we do not make house calls. "Well here's the thing, I am a nudist and if I try and go to your office I get arrested if I have nothing on." "I understand, you will need to put some clothes on for your visit to our office." This strange conversation continues as he explains that that is not going to work for him. "It completely Jacks up my groove and I just can't do it" he says. "Okay, thank you for calling" I say.

I am hoping he will take the hint and hang the hell up.

"Do you have any labs that are only for nudists" he asks me. "No sir we sure don't. Maybe my supervisor can help you?" I suggest. I give him Sheryl's number and he seems satisfied. I need to go check the calendar to see if it is a full moon? Yep, full moon tonight. I had a feeling. I am going to remind Sheryl about getting us a Valium salt lick for our waiting room. I think that just may be the solution.

I decide to call Sheryl right now. When Sheryl picks up the phone she sounds a bit irritated and I start to lose my nerve, but regain it quickly. "Hi Sheryl, this is Betty in Whitney Park. I think I have a partial solution to some of our problems here in Whitney Park." "You don't say?" Sheryl says. "Do tell." "Well, as you know it is a full moon right now and I think we could use a Valium salt lick here in the waiting room." After the laughing stops she says "how very astute of you to pick up on that Betty. I will get on it right away." Followed by more laughing as she hangs up.

I hang up and grab the other line that is ringing. "SuperLab, this is Betty." "Yes, young lady, I have a lab slip here and I need to come in to get my blood drawn." "Okay" I say. "Is there a time that I can come in when it is less crowded?" "I have no idea, we just never know how many patients will be here at any given time." Then he asks if I am any good at drawing blood? "No not really" I tell him "your best bet is to go to the main lab in Misty and ask for Bill. He is the best phlebotomist around, everyone loves him. "Well I think I will do just that" he says. "Yes tell him Betty sent you." I snicker to myself thinking of him asking for Bill.

Only one more hour to go and I have no idea what Steffy is up to? I am going to call Liz to see what she is doing but before I can dial her number the phone rings. A full moon, means you dread answering the phones. "SuperLab, this is Betty." "Oh thank goodness you answered" the familiar voice says. "Well hello Mrs. Brown how are you today?" "Honey, I am so excited. I have made arrangements for my house to be moved." "Oh Really? Where are they moving it to?" I ask. "Well here is the thing, there is no real address. It is out in the desert by mile marker one hundred and fifty two, off of highway twenty four."

"Are you planning on living there in the house out in the desert?" I ask. "Yes, it is on a piece of land called BLM land and nobody bothers you." I ask her if she will have power and television and she tells me not right away but that she will figure out something.

"I will just be happy to have my house all to myself. Marty can keep the land the house used to be on for now and of course the pink garage." "Mrs. Brown, this sounds kind of extreme? Do you feel safe? Do you have any neighbors?"

"Well, right now it might be a little scary at night with no power, but I have my gun for protection. Oh and I can practice shooting my gun out there because there is nothing around. Honey, my house is so clean now." Good grief, the thought of this old lady out in the middle of nowhere is scary.

"Guess what?" she says "I cleaned out our bank accounts this morning. I left him one dollar for every year we were married in both the checking and saving account, so he has forty two dollars in each account." "Wow Mrs. Brown, that is very generous of you." "Right! That is exactly what I thought too. Damn generous in fact. I also left all his tools in the garage for him so he should be quite happy. He can host his poker games out there, although he may miss having a bathroom."

Mrs. Brown continues with her story and tells me that she

went back to the gun store and bought some life size targets that resemble a person so that she can really practice shooting her gun. Marty and his buddy Fred should be back in about ten days.

Next Mrs. Brown starts telling me that Fred's' wife just called and said she was driving home from the supermarket and noticed the house was gone? Mrs. Brown said she explained to her that she was surprising Marty, so best not to mention it to Fred when he calls. She seemed a bit puzzled but agreed to keep the secret. Mrs. Brown says that Fred's' wife most likely would not understand and would think she was crazy, which she is very sure she is not.

I have no idea how Mrs. Brown has been able to pull this off but she sure is one gutsy old broad. She is seventy six years old and seems to have few if any fears. I hope I am that way when and if I live to be here age.

Well, this crazy day is just about over. Spoke too soon, the phone is ringing and it is four fifty p.m. I pick up the phone. "Hi this is Marty Brown. I am having no luck reaching my wife and I was wondering if she comes in for blood work can you tell her I am trying to reach her?" "Yes, I absolutely will." He thanks me and we hang up.

I couldn't very well tell him that he is never going to be able to get a hold of her. I am starting to feel sorry for the poor old guy. I hope she left his personal things in the garage, because forty two dollars will not get him very far.

Time to lock the door. I am so excited about leaving that I trip and nearly kill myself rushing to lock the door. I am planning to go home and just veg and watch tv. I don't want to see or talk to anyone tonight. I think I will stop for some Chinese food for dinner on my way home. Tomorrow is another day.

CHAPTER

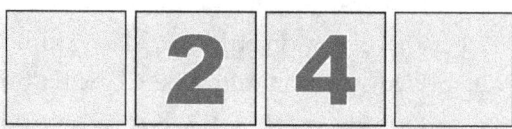

OH BOY, RIGHT IN THE MIDDLE OF A DREAM about the Prize Patrol coming to my door when the alarm goes off and I realize the whole thing is a dream. I am so sad. Back to reality.

Time to get into the shower, get dressed and get myself over to Whitney Park. Just thinking about going to work gives me a stomach ache. Well, if I don't get going I won't have a job and then I won't have a place to live. A friend of mine told me she cannot believe how excited I get over the lottery and how I actually expect to win. Duh, I am not spending all this money hoping to lose.

As I pull into the parking lot a feeling of dread comes over me. This seems to be happening more often than before. As I head down the hall to the lab I see about ten people in line. "Good morning everyone" I say cheerfully as I unlock the door and hold it open for the first few patients. "I was technically before you" a woman tells the one in front of her.

"I hardly think so. I had to move back a little for the lady to open the door." "Well nobody forced you to move." And so my day at SuperLab begins.

Everyone is signing in as I get the lights and machines turned on so I can start registering people. The phone is ringing already. "SuperLab" I say as I pick it up. It is Mary in Urgent Care telling me they have a draw. "Okay Mary, Liz will be here in twenty minutes and I can send her down. "But we need somebody right now" she says. "I am all alone with ten patients standing here waiting for me to draw their blood Mary." "Okay, let me see what the doctor wants to do" she says. We hang up.

"Mr. Thomas, are you fasting?" "No. Nobody said anything about fasting to me. Why didn't anybody tell me this before?" I tell him that I am really sorry nobody told him about the fasting requirements before he storms out. I cross his name off the list on the clip board and get ready to call the next patient as the phone rings. "SuperLab may I help you?" "Well I hope so, I need some labs done." I proceed to answer all of the gentleman's questions, give him our address, directions and hours when he says that he has more questions. I ask him to please hold and go back to my patient.

Liz walks in and I ask her if she can grab the call on line one? She puts her stuff away and I hear her respond to the man on the phone "ummm yes sir those are our real hours." "That other lady was very rude" he says. Liz is silent. "Are you there?" "Yes sir, but if you have no more questions I must hang up now." Click, the line is dead, he hung up on Liz.

I remind Liz that when she gets a chance she should *check the specimen*?

We both are drawing blood now so the line is going down

quickly. Nine twenty a.m. and Steffy has just arrived.

Today Steffy has blue hair, blue nails and an eerie looking blue lipstick that makes her look cyanotic. A medical term for deprived of oxygen. Of course this all matches her blue scrubs and blue shoes. "Good morning Steffy, can you jump in and help us draw? "Yep" she says and she calls Mrs. Nelson back.

I hear Mrs. Nelson asking Steffy about her blue hair. "Wasn't your hair black a while ago?" she asks. "Probably" Steffy says. "Look lady, what's up with all the questions?" "I am just making conversation young lady. I only want to be stuck once and I will tell you where to stick your needle." "I don't think so" says Steffy. "I will get you a different phlebotomist." So Steffy walks out to the front and announces that she needs somebody to draw Mrs. Nelson. Liz and I do rock/paper/scissors.

Lucky Liz gets to draw Mrs. Nelson's blood. I can hear Liz getting her supplies ready and Mrs. Nelson starting her usual spiel about only one try. "I will stick you once where I feel the best vein is, period" Liz says. Mrs. Nelson says "never mind, I will go to the main lab." Liz wishes her well and tells her to ask for Sheryl. Mrs. Nelson mumbled something about never returning to this office again as she walks out. We should be so lucky, I would personally be thrilled if we never saw her again.

Liz walks out and asks me to *check the specimen* when I get time. I disappear into the break room. What a surprise, Liz just used the Z on a triple letter and then the whole word was doubled. I am entertaining thoughts of strangling her. I do have the Q so all I need to do is really study the board and figure out how to maximize the letters to get me the most points.

As I walk out of the break room Steffy is telling Liz a new story about why she had to change her hair and nails to blue and how much her boyfriend loves this color. Liz looks bored to tears and keeps yawning. Steffy tells Liz that her boyfriend got a car instead of the motorcycle, so now they can go on dates if it is raining. Liz just nods and says oh really?

I head to the processing room. I cannot bear to listen to one more story. It looks like we are all caught up so I slip out the back door of the processing room to get some fresh air. Hopefully when I walk back inside I will have a new perspective on things.

As I walk back into the lab there is a male patient talking to Liz about his stool collection process. She gives him the vials and a container to collect the stools in at home. He is telling her he wants to collect them here at the lab and be done with it. She is trying to convince him that collection at home is much better. He is not playing along and the next thing we know he is heading to the bathroom. Unfortunately this means that the other patients will all be lined up outside the bathroom door waiting to be able to collect their urine. This is so gross and offensive. Each time we get a patient like this I want to scream. Is it five o'clock yet?

The phone rings and I head to the front to answer it. Answering the phone is better than dealing with the idiot with the stool containers.

"SuperLab" I say. "Yes, hello I am trying to find you, are you near the donut shop? I am almost to the signal and when the traffic begins to move I will be able to see what street I am on. Can you hold on a bit?"

I am out of patience with these idiotic questions so I announce that I am going to lunch. I am going to go hit some tennis balls and hopefully work off some stress. After hitting tennis balls for thirty minutes I am starving. I am going back and forth in mind about taking the time to shower down in Urgent Care in the on call room. I decide I don't feel like it and really don't care if I stink. Instead I stop at a Mexican restaurant for a super burrito.

This will improve my mood and get me through the rest of the day. I call Liz to see if she wants one? Pork for her. I am going to take my sweet time. The thought of going back to the looney bin is too much.

"Ma'am it is going to take a bit longer today as we have a new cook" says the lady behind the counter at the restaurant. "No problem, I have all day" I tell her. I will sample all of the salsas while I wait. I scoop up some chips and start dipping. I am daydreaming that I am down in Cabo on the beach when the girl taps me on the shoulder to get my attention, my order is ready.

I am a long way from Cabo. I thank her and head back to the loony bin. As I walk in I head straight to the back room, Liz joins me and we dig in. We discuss how burned out we are as we eat our burritos. Liz wants to switch to two days a week and she is going to talk to her husband about it. I wish I had that option.

Liz blurts out that we have been in there for forty five minutes and we have no idea what Steffy is doing? Liz goes out first to check. Steffy is in the back on her cell phone and there are three patients waiting. Seriously? I guess we have to watch this idiot constantly.

Liz is up front registering patients and I go and check things in the processing room. Tubes of blood are still sitting in the rack so I get them into the centrifuge. The phones are both ringing and Liz puts them on hold. I guess I am obligated to answer, but if I get one more stupid question today I may explode and say something awful.

"Thank you for waiting, may I help you?" "Um yes, can you please give me your hours?" I tell her that we are open Monday through Friday from eight to five and Saturday from nine to two. "Oh okay, so you are open until five today?" Why can't people just listen.

I answer line two, praying that just this once I will get a normal person, and say "thank you for waiting, may I help you?"

"Hi my name is Debbie, I have a unique problem and I need someone to come out to my house to draw my blood." "I'm sorry we do not make house calls." "I have a fear of leaving my house, I have not left my house in over two years" she tells me. "Maybe if you call our main lab and ask for Bill he can help you" I say. I recite the phone number and wish her good luck. This should make Bills' day.

I head to the front room and I see Cedrik urinating on the front of the building. I mention to Liz that he is here. She rolls her eyes as she gathers her things and gives me the goodbye greeting "see ya wouldn't want to be ya." Today I am able to laugh out loud.

As Cedrik stumbles in the door I can see he forgot to zip his fly again. I will put Steffy's name on the requisition. I ask him how his wife is doing? He tells me she moved out. Awkward. I say sorry to hear that and I hear Steffy call him to the back. Steffy tells him that his fly is open and he ignores her. Fifteen minutes later he stumbles out the door. I am surprised Steffy was able to get his blood because he is a slightly difficult draw. I wonder how many holes he has in his arms from her trying to get the blood?

I head down to Primary Care to deliver results. Cindy

greets me at the front desk and says "I saw Steffy the other day and seriously she looks really scary." "Yes I think it scares the patients also" I tell her. I walk back into the office, there are three patients signed in and no sign of Steffy.

I decide to try something new and I walk to her room where she draws the blood. She is playing on her phone. I walk over and lay down on the exam table. Less than a minute later she walks out. Perfect, I don't know why I never thought of this before? I hear her calling a patient up to the window and I decide I will just lie here and let her register everyone. This is awesome. I hear both phone lines ringing, do I move? Of course not, let's see what Steffy is made of?

Fifteen minutes later I head up front and call a patient back to draw their blood. I was doing some thinking back there about how I wish I had a better job. Unfortunately wishing will not make it so.

I call a Mr. Watkins back. "Good afternoon sir." He says hello but is not talkative. I wonder if this is Mr. Browns' friend? First name is Fred. Do I dare ask? Mr. Watkins is wearing a faded Hawaiian shirt, shorts and filthy shoes. How are you today Mr. Watkins? He grunts and says not very well. "Oh I see" I say.

I just got back early from a fishing trip with my friend Marty. His wife moved his house while he was gone. "You don't say." "All he has left is a garage." "Oh no, what is he going to do?" "I don't know. I guess he will be using our bathroom or putting in an outhouse. His wife is a crazy woman and he is looking for her and his house." Geez I better get him out of here. I pick a twenty gauge needle because it is a bit bigger and the tubes will fill faster. I tell him to take care as I tape his arm.

As I walk out behind him with the tubes of blood I notice that Steffy is putting more makeup on at the front desk. I keep going to the processing room. I start the centrifuge and head out the side door inside the processing room. As I head through the doors to the lobby of Urgent Care I see Mary who is one of the nurses there. She is dealing with another fun scene. Yep whatever is in the drinking water at Whitney Park affects them too.

There is a young mother who put her four kids in one of those beach wagons and as she turned the corner the wagon tipped over and now she has four children crying on the floor in the lobby. Too much fun. I pretend to be on my phone as I go by so I do not have to stop.

I take a deep breath as I walk outside. I wish I could just get in my car and leave. I think I will call Liz and see what she is up to? Liz sounds relaxed. She is eating ice cream and watching tv. I tell her about Fred Watkins coming in after I remind her who he is. "Really?" she says. "Yep. He told me Marty is looking for his house. Seriously, why do we get such weird freaking people in our lab?" Liz asks me if Sheryl thought the Valium salt lick was a good idea? "What was her reaction?" "She Laughed" I said.

As we are chatting I see a Toyota four door pulling into the parking lot. Next I notice there is a police officer with his lights on behind a little old lady. I tell Liz. She is driving all through the parking lot looking for the perfect spot and she has no idea the cop is behind her. I seriously hope I don't live past seventy two. Finally she finds her spot. As she exits the car she still does not see him. He walks up to her and stops her. Geez it is Mrs. Brown. She is back at the car looking for her registration. Oh my I hope she has her gun safely put away.

I see him looking in the glove box as she sits down in the driver's seat. Okay he is writing her a ticket so hopefully he will be gone shortly. She must have run the stop sign at the corner. I think I will sneak back inside and wait for her arrival.

As I walk back into the office I notice there is a strong perfume like smell. "Steffy, what is that smell?" "Oh just some perfume. I thought I would freshen up, so I am ready for my big evening. John is taking me out for dinner." "Oh Really?" I say. "It is a fancy restaurant called Sizzler." I try and keep a straight face. She asks me if I have ever been there and if she is dressed all right? Sizzler is an old steakhouse chain restaurant where you can wear anything at all. Where has this girl been? I just say yes.

The door opens and it is Mrs. Brown. I move into the chair and greet her as she walks up to the window. "Hi Mrs. Brown how are you?" I say. "Fine dear, I am not here for labs. I just want to talk to you." "Oh okay come on back." I take her into the break room. She Laughs when she sees the Scrabble game.

I tell her she just missed Fred Watkins by less than an hour. "Oh really?" she says. "I guess that means Marty is back and has noticed the house is gone." "Well he would have to be blind not to notice" I offer. "Honey, there's a slight problem with my plan." "Really?" I say. "The tax bill came today and needs to be paid in like two months. I am trying to decide what to do with it?"

"I can't really pay half of it and get Marty to pay the other half because all he has is the land and the garage right?" I suggest that she call him and talk about it. Actually he might pay half because if he doesn't he will not even have the land and the garage to live in. "Very good point," she says. She dials

Marty on her phone and he picks up on the first ring. I can hear him from where I am standing. "Where are you? Where is our damn house?" She tells him she will call back when he is in a better mood. He was still yelling when she hung up. They say people change during retirement.

Whew look at the time, it is almost time for me to go home. "Well all right dear I shall be on my way. I have to get back before dark so I can find my house." "Okay be careful Mrs. Brown" I say. "I will dear, see you soon."

I head to the front to see what Steffy is up to? She is sitting at the front desk looking at herself in her compact mirror. I go check the processing room to make sure everything is ready for the courier. I get ready to lock the door and get my stuff together when Steffy's man walks in. I tell her to go ahead and go. He is wearing a pair of shorts and flip flops. I hope he has a shirt in the car? I don't think even Sizzler will serve him without a shirt.

I am going to check to see when my vacation is? I need a break from this office. As I head out to my car I make a mental note to see where I could go on a week long vacation.

Today is payday. I am checking to see if my check is in my bank account and to see if my raise is on there. Uh huh I think it is in there. Unbelievable, what tiny amount of money I get for this important job. What a joke.

As I drive home I contemplate what I might do with a week off? Perhaps I should wait until I save enough money to actually go somewhere? In the back of my mind is crazy Mrs. Brown, I still cannot believe she actually moved the house.

CHAPTER

2 5

WOW SIX THIRTY A.M. ALREADY? I can hardly wait to see what will happen at the loony bin today?

Usually I walk around to the side of the Urgent Care office because I arrive before the main doors to the Whitney Health Center are open. Today I just sit in my car and sip my coffee until they unlock the front doors and I can walk in the main entrance. Most likely there are patients for the lab already waiting in line arguing with each other over how many minutes late I am. The more things change, the more they stay the same. I feel tired just thinking of the day ahead.

I make my way into the building and head down the hall to the lab. I never know when I walk down the hallway what kind of disaster I will find? As I head down the hall I pause at the double doors to the lab to see what the patients are doing? Two women towards the front of the line are brushing each others hair. A couple of people are on their laptop computers and phones and there is a male patient curled up in a ball asleep while staying in line. I will never understand why these patients come so early just to wait in line. Once I open the door there will be another wait while I set up the office and start registering patients. The smarter patients come in after nine a.m. when there are generally three phlebotomists drawing blood.

As the patients' begin to sign in the phones are already ringing off the hook. I answer the first line and I cannot believe what I am hearing. On the other end of the line a woman is telling me that I won a contest that I entered. Now I buy a lot of lottery tickets and enter a lot of contests so I have no idea which contest this woman was talking about. I almost fall off my chair when I hear that I have won a free trip for two to Hawaii.

My first thought is that someone is playing a sick joke on me. After hearing more of the details and remembering actually entering this contest at a recent local event I begin to realize this is really happening. I have actually won this trip.

Inside I am jumping up and down with joy. The trip is for two people. Who shall I bring?

On the outside I am trying to act normal and act like I actually care. "Yes ma'am I do care deeply about how you are feeling. Yes, I will get busy drawing blood as soon as possible" I tell the woman staring at me at the front counter while my mind is racing with excitement.

You have got to be kidding me! This bird is flying the coop for ten days and as soon as possible. I am thinking I should make it a double whammy for the lab and take Liz with me. I wonder if we can leave within a couple days. We can have ten mental health days on the beach in Hawaii. I can not believe this is really happening.

Now what to tell management? How will Sheryl take both of us being gone for two weeks at the same time? I could always use the old *family emergency* excuse. Maybe Liz can use a *death in the family* excuse? Of course we could try telling her the truth and take our chances.

Oh goody Liz has just arrived. She doesn't seem to be in a very good mood this morning, well I am about to change that. I can't wait to tell her the exciting news.

A few weeks go by and Liz and I are actually heading to the airport. We were able to work out all the details at home, in fact my son Jared and his girlfriend are thrilled to have the house to themselves for ten days. I think Liz's husband is also happy for the break.

At work we actually decided to tell Sheryl the truth about me winning the trip and we were able to schedule the time off after promising to not only put up with Steffy when we return but also help and train her as much as possible.

One thing is for sure, the worst day in Hawaii will be better than the best day at work. It is definitely time for us to take a real mental health vacation and run off into the sunset. Aloha!

www.ingramcontent.com/pod-product-compliance
Lightning Source LLC
Chambersburg PA
CBHW071236250626
47163CB00001B/204